Her Day to Die

A Dark Why Choose
Sage RelleAnne

Rainbow Publishing House LLC

Paperback ISBN: 979-8-9910037-3-5

Proofread by Anna Lisa Vitale and Ashleigh Voros of Split Leaf Saturdays book editing

Edited by: **Cal LaBorde**

Cover by Krafigs Designs

First Edition 2024

Contents

Introduction

Hi y'all,

This has gone through several rounds of editing and a round of proof-reading. If anything still managed to slip through, please let me know. My email is sagerelleanne@gmail.com

If you have not read anything by me yet, a few things before you buckle into this wild ride.

I write in both first and third person. This will be pretty consistent among all of my novels. For this one Sunday is in first POV and the men will be in third.

Most have loved this, but some have **not**.

Now that, that's out of the way, thank you so very kindly for giving my book a read. I greatly appreciate your support!

Okay I promise that's everything (besides the triggers).

VERY IMPORTANT

This book has quite a few trigger warnings.

For an extensive in-depth list please reach out to me at: sagerelleanne@g

mail.com

Brief outline of triggers:

Mentions of drug use and abuse

Mentions of SA (not graphic or to FMC)

Murder

Loss of loved ones (not the main characters)

Cliffhanger - this is a planned duet

Blood and gore

Acknowledgements

To my loving husband.

Your grief from the loss of your brother is something I witnessed very close hand.

Your strength and perseverance are admirable.

You inspire me every.

Single.

Day.

Dedication

To every person that has lost someone near and dear to your heart.

I hope your grief does not drown you.

I hope you find your equivalent to the O'Brien brothers.

Someone or something to keep you safe while you navigate the waters of a world without that person by your side.

May you find your own peace.

Prologue

JUNE 1st

They're both dead.

Part I Denial and Anger

June 13th

The bathtub isn't clean.

That's my first thought as I balance myself under the shower's spray waiting for the water to heat up, ignoring the chill that settles into my bones.

I feel sick, uneasy, wobbly. As if everything I have ever known could be popped at any moment.

The now hot mist bounces off my naked form and catches in my eyes. I push the tub's lever and turn the drizzle to a steady stream coming from the faucet. I slowly lower myself and lay back. As the water gradually fills up around my form, I am waiting for my release.

The stopper is an old thing, and I grab a washcloth from the ledge and move it to wedge into the drain for good measure. I am impatient. I need to complete this ritual before I lose myself. My vision spins a bit as I lay back down, waiting for the water to fill.

Finally, it touches my ears. I take a deep breath and shut my eyes as it covers my cheeks, my mouth, my eyes, my nose. Once I am fully submerged I use my foot to shut the water off prior to it overflowing onto the floor below. And then I relax.

Underneath the water I no longer feel so empty, so lost, so full of anxiety. I am simply existing on the cusp of something that could be both a beginning and an ending.

I float in this ethereal moment for as long as I can, enjoying the control it provides me. I imagine myself at the space center, the first time I joined Tripp and Auggie on an excursion. Tripp lived next door to me my whole life, but we had never hung out together before. I didn't expect him to be so sweet, kind, and caring. The entire day I spent with my cheeks flushed and my heart attempting to escape its confines.

When my lungs begin to protest, I pretend as if I can breathe underwater. I push my chest in and out in the mimicry of breath. It works for a few more moments to trick my body into believing I am actually giving it what it needs. I remember almost tumbling down the old stairs and Tripp catching me. The firm grip of his hands on my hips. Falling into the security of his warmth.

It doesn't last nearly long enough. After a few more replications, I am forced to exhale the air in my lungs and push myself out of the water.

Forced to come to the realization that I no longer have anyone to go to the planetarium at the space center with. That there's no one to catch me when I fall.

I hear screaming coming from down the hall and realize that no amount of escape can keep me from this reality. My parents are at it again.

Every night exactly like this since Auggie's death.

I quickly towel off and throw on comfortable clothes. I lift open my window and swing myself out and up. I use the ledge as leverage to push myself onto the roof.

The moon is absent, but the stars are my true goal. This was where Tripp and I would go to escape our day-to-day lives. Our families. Our responsibilities. Our realities.

This was where he promised he would wait for me, that we would last the one year apart. This was where I told him I loved him.

I stop the line of thought; I can't go down this memory lane again. Instead, I lay back and look at the stars.

After a few minutes, the roof next door catches my attention. It's where Tripp lived. Along with his brothers. Even Auggie would spend most of his time there growing up, but he never brought me along.

Movement on the roof has me squinting my eyes. I almost expect to see Auggie and Tripp, but whatever it is, I completely forget as brightness shrouds the night sky.

I return my attention to the sky just as it dulls and a single star begins to fall.

A shooting star.

I make a wish.

I wish to reunite with the ones I love.

Auggie, my brother. Tripp, my first love.

Guilt furrows deep in my belly and I don't give Tripp's roof any more attention... he isn't up there.

I am alone.

Tripp and Auggie are dead.

And it is my fault.

June 14th

It's raining. Coming down in painful, small piercing pebbles, but I pay it no mind. They decided to have the memorial outside in the middle of the summer. Who's bright idea was that?

And why is it for the both of them? Do Auggie and Tripp not deserve their own individual time to be mourned?

I am seated on a plastic white chair in the front row to a makeshift stand. The row reserved for family. Across a small gap is another column of chairs. I am one of the last stragglers still enduring the weather. The priest declared we would move the *celebration* inside. A celebration of life. What a joke. What is there to celebrate? Two people are dead.

Auggie and Tripp, why did you have to leave me behind?

Fuck.

Loneliness settles into my gut, a well that is slowly filling to the brim. My skin feels tight against my bones as I shift in my seat.

Blinking through the rain, I realize that I am in fact not alone. Across the gap, and in the front row, are three boys.

Correction–three men.

Three men that are not crying. They are not showing any emotion except what appears to be annoyance.

As if this entire memorial is just an inconvenience to the lot of them.

I always knew they were awful but Tripp tried to convince me otherwise. We never spent much time around each other, but they had never seemed to like me. It didn't bother me though.

I didn't particularly like them either.

If only Tripp could see his brothers now...

I bet he wouldn't even be bothered.

That was the kind of man Tripp was. Sweet, understanding, caring. It is what made me fall so hard for him. Why I pursued him even when I knew he would be heading off to college and leaving me behind.

I never even had the chance to tell Auggie about us. Tripp and I were going to break the news together. We wanted to wait until I had graduated, until I was eighteen, to soften the blow of me dating one of his best friends.

My tears mix with the rain. The dichotomy of cold and warm streams down my face. If only I hadn't pressured them to come. If only we didn't have to keep everything hidden.

If only. *If only.*

I watch as the three men in the row across from mine exchange a look. Less than a moment later, they eerily turn the weight of their gazes to me.

Do they know I am the reason their brother decided to make the trip here? Do they blame me just as I blame myself?

I can't tell anything from their eyes and I avert my own before I can let the guilt reflect on my face.

Grayson, Darius, and Axel. The three remaining O'Brien brothers. The ones I had always avoided like the plague. Axel and Tripp may have been twins but they could not be any more different. Even still, I can't stand to look at Axel, and for a moment, I find it hard to breathe. They look exactly alike but that is where the similarities end.

Axel's stint in prison ended just in time to hear the news of his brother's death. Just in time to make it to this joke of a memorial. Whereas Tripp went to college on an academic scholarship, Axel was arrested on battery charges and tried as an adult.

Darius wasn't so bad, except he decided one day about two months ago, right after his eighteenth birthday, to just up and drop out of high school. Did he foresee that the eve of our graduation would end in this tragedy?

I certainly hadn't.

And Grayson? Well, I never could get a read on the eldest O'Brien brother, but his harsh features weren't doing any favors for my opinion.

"Sunday, get your ass inside!" My mother's voice pierces through the storm that is both brewing internally and externally.

I pay no more mind to the O'Brien brothers as I gather myself and as much energy as I can to steady my emotions. I'm not sure how I am supposed to go on. Not without Auggie. Not without Tripp.

Fuck.

Finally, I find my footing and stand haphazardly up from the soaked plastic chair. The rain has intensified and both my clothes and hair are plastered down.

I permit myself one more moment of misery as I step into the cathedral filled with sympathetic strangers, attempting to pay no more attention to the brothers in my wake, even as I feel the weight of their stares on my back. There is something incredibly off-putting about the remaining O'Briens.

About their uniform unwavering attention. About their emotionless display at their brother's memorial. About the way it almost feels as if they are waiting for me... to do *something*.

But what?

A terrifying feeling creeps down my spine. It takes a moment to recognize it, but once I do, I can't shake it. It sinks into my skin, causes my heart to beat into my ears, my fingers to shake.

Apprehension.

I make it my mission then and there to avoid the brothers as best I can.

June 14th

S haking off my uneasiness, I glance around the space for any familiar faces.

Carrie, my friend, isn't here, but I don't expect her to be. She and my brother did not end on the best of terms and our friendship fizzled after their breakup. However, Veronica, Auggie's most recent girlfriend, is also noticeably missing. I want to be angry by her absence, but I can't blame her.

This memorial is a joke.

I find myself wishing more than anything that my best friend, Julia, was here. But she's not, she's been fading from my life for months.

I'm here alone.

The plop of rain drops falls to the floor around me in a puddle. But even that is not enough to ward off the sympathetic arm pats. Not enough to dispel the cloud of cheap perfume as I am pulled into numbing hugs.

I question once more the fairness of a world that would sooner take my brother than me. Auggie was always so full of life and promise. He would know how to navigate the waters of today. He would know what to say to our parents as they fought over blame.

And what about Tripp? What about his brothers? They were raised by a grandmother who recently passed away. I had never heard of their father, and their mother wasn't much of the parenting type.

Glancing around, I realize she isn't even here.

Tripp had explained his mother to me once. He summed it up quite well.

She loves us boys the only way she can, by not corrupting us with herself.

I find myself suddenly angry. Livid. Raging. As if the rain is no longer chilling me to the bone but somehow manages to set me on fire. As if it isn't water at all, but gasoline.

I give a tight-lipped smile to the priest who had been talking *at* me for the last several minutes. "Excuse me," I rudely cut through whatever bullshit he's spewing and make my way to my parents.

"Sunday." My mother's voice holds a tone of warning.

My father remains silent, he simply leans back against the wall, the beer in his hand a testament to how loud their fight will be tonight.

"I came as promised. I need to change." I try to calm my swell of emotion and gesture to the water that still drips down from me onto the floor.

"How do you expect to get home?" My mother's words are shrill. Grating.

"Carrie said she can pick me up." The lie comes out shockingly easily.

My mother doesn't look convinced, but before she can say anything, a sturdy muscular arm lands around my shoulders. A broad hand fanning across my bare skin.

"I'll take her Mrs. Masch." *Grayson.*

His deep voice is unmistakable, but I don't shake off the unwanted savior's touch, even as I stiffen from his words.

Why the fuck would he take me anywhere?

His presence alone is more soothing than it has any right being. As if he has comforted me a hundred times before, except he hasn't. My brain and heart are at war as I find myself subconsciously leaning into him for borrowed strength.

Even though I just vowed to avoid his very existence.

Even though I can't understand why he is standing here offering me a ride home.

My mother flashes a sympathetic smile at the man whose arm still holds me tightly. "Grayson, sweetheart, I told you to call me Joan. And you poor boys, you know if you need anything to let me know. Are you sure taking Sunday won't be a hassle?"

I start to argue that I wouldn't be going anywhere with this man, but his hand on my skin squeezes, causing me to gasp instead.

My mother pays it no mind, her attention solely focused on Grayson.

"None at all." Grayson's grip does not lessen as he speaks the words.

I don't have any chance to argue as Grayson drags me away from my parents and back outside.

The downpour has only intensified, the wind has picked up, and lightning shoots across the sky, but I find it oddly cathartic.

Grayson halts any further movement, and we remain shielded from the onslaught by a patio above. My mind finally catches up to what is going on, and suddenly, I feel suffocated by the behemoth of a man. I need space from him. Why is he here? What can he possibly want from me?

I attempt to jerk out of his restraints, but as if he expected it, Grayson uses his free hand to snatch up and keep me in place. His long fingers overlap around my wrist, but still, I refuse to look him in the eyes. My stomach is churning uncomfortably and I cannot exactly pinpoint how I am feeling.

But there is one thing I know for certain; he makes me feel small. Insignificant. Childlike. Controlled.

I squirm, trying to break free from his clutches as panic takes over all rational thought.

"Stop struggling!" Grayson loudly grunts at me over the noise of the storm.

I want to argue, but a flash of light has me pausing my verbal assault.

Lightning strikes the ground a dozen yards from where we stand. Exactly on the path I would have taken home. It is so close to us that the ground shakes and the air is filled with static. My ears are ringing as I look down at Grayson's hand on me. His hold is what stopped me from being a crispy pile on the sidewalk.

From dying at a memorial.

How did he know to stop me?

Apprehension once more slinks down my spine and I finally meet my captor's eyes. Except in this moment, he is also my savior.

Unruly sienna hair half covers his hazel eyes, but even still, I can make out the fear that is reflected there.

He's afraid of something?

This time when I jerk back, he lets me go.

Grayson crosses muscular arms over a broad chest. His black suit hides most of his skin, save for his hands. His broad hands are covered in tattoos and scars. He shifts and reaches up to rub nervously at his trimmed beard along his strong jaw, for just a moment, before recrossing his arms.

This man isn't safe. He's older, more intelligent, larger. Everything about his presence screams danger. It yells that I need to run. That he wants to hurt me. That he knows why his brother is dead. That he'll exact his revenge for my role in his death.

Grayson clears his throat, and I jerk my investigation away from his arms, up and up and up, eventually resettling on his eyes.

The fear there has been replaced by a cockiness that snaps me back to reality.

"Like what you see?" His sarcastic tone shakes off the last of my concern.

"No." My hands are still shaking from my near death, but I am done with this interaction, done with this man.

The terror from the lightning is long forgotten and now I just want to peel out of these clothes and go back to my bathtub. Then maybe if the rain stops I can fall asleep on the roof. Under the stars.

A shadow crosses Grayson's face and this time he catches me by the shoulders before I have the intent to move. "That's what you always say." His words are barely audible and they don't make any sense.

I haven't had many interactions with Grayson. We aren't friends. We aren't even enemies. We just avoid each other.

He is the brother of the man I loved. He is—was—one of my brother's best friends. All of the O'Briens were. Grayson is my neighbor. That is it. Except, the way his eyes are scrutinizing me now makes me think there's something I'm missing.

I don't like this feeling. As if I am the butt of some cosmic prank, and once more, unexpected anger furls deep in my belly. "Is this some kind of joke? I know you are grieving too, but please just leave me alone. Thanks for saving me from the lightning, but I just want to go home."

I attempt to pull from his grip, but he does not allow my escape.

He's still just staring cryptically into my eyes as if wishing for me to understand an inside joke I was never privy to.

I can't handle this. I can't deal with this scrutiny. Doesn't he understand I need to be away from people? That I'm trying to run away, not be stared down? I just want to lose myself in peace.

"Let her go," the familiar soft but stern voice comes from over my shoulder. It's Darius, the youngest brother.

The noise startles Grayson out of whatever trance he had gone into, and he lets go of me. Suddenly. I'm falling backwards.

Directly into another man's chest.

"Easy there."

I recognize Axel's voice, but I don't say anything. He sounds almost exactly like—I don't complete the thought. I can't. Instead, I yank free from his arms, the leather of his jacket scratching me as I do, and sprint away.

I stop my retreat halfway across the parking lot and turn my head. All three of the brothers are once more watching me.

I know in my gut that something isn't right, but I don't have the where-withal to care.

I don't want to be around these strangers anymore. I am alone and anyone who made me feel differently is gone.

June 19th

*E*verything is white. I try to blink a few times or even move, but I can't control anything. I can't feel anything. Except, inexplicably, I know for certain if I could, I would be in pain.

Am I dead?

After a moment, I hear the muted sound of retreating feet shuffling against carpet, and then a door opening and closing.

But still, all I see is white, as if it is pressed into my very eyeballs.

"Oh, Sunflower."

Suddenly I am being shifted, now I can see that the world has not been reduced to whiteness. I am in a room I don't recognize, and right in front of me, staring into my very soul, are a set of emerald eyes.

I want to reach out, to say something, but I can't. I am frozen, but that does not change the misery that hangs heavily in my heart.

"It's going to be okay, you're going to wake up and this will all just be a nightmare." Tripp pulls me forward into his arms, the move jostles me so that I can now see another figure in the room.

"Hey there sis, what did I tell you about trying drugs? About parties?"

Confusion and sadness sweep through me as equal waves in my heart.

"Stop it, she won't understand. Give her more time." Tripp's words are raspy, saturated in hopelessness.

I want more than anything to tell these men how much I miss them. That I love them. That I need *them.*

I can see as something shifts across my brother's face. "But that's the problem isn't it? No matter how much time she has, she never learns." He reaches forward ruffling my hair. His words don't make any sense to me, but I can't speak to question him. "Love you sis, it's going to be okay. Just follow your gut and be careful who you trust."

My vision fades, and suddenly, there are a thousand spiders crawling across my skin and leaving a trail of agony in their wake.

I don't know why, but I wake up screaming.

The sound pierces the otherwise silent space, but nobody comes to check on me.

I am alone.

Even worse than that, it's my birthday.

I roll back over, further into my pillows trying to find some sort of comfort.

It's been five days since the memorial, and I haven't left my house since. I have barely even left my bed. I haven't seen either of my parents; they work at the hospital and are rarely home. I wouldn't know they existed except for their periodic fighting.

I feel so incredibly numb and lost. I had my entire life planned, and in less than a moment, it was snuffed out. I will no longer be starting college this year, I will not be showing off my boyfriend, I won't be rooming with my best friend, Julia, I won't be escaping this town like so many do.

I am stuck.

Tendrils of unexpected jealousy creep into my heart; Auggie and Tripp aren't forced to go through this. They left me all alone to pick up the pieces.

The thought leaves me feeling guilty, but it doesn't make it any less true.

Rage slithers across my body. Heats my skin. Prickles my nerves.

I want to scream, rage, and destroy everything in my sight. Instead, I pull my blankets back over my head.

A nagging feeling has squirmed its way into my gut; shame. I will allow myself one more day to stew. But tomorrow, I will live. If not for myself, then for Auggie and Tripp.

Today was the day Tripp and I were going to announce our relationship. We figured being a legal adult would numb the blow. That Auggie would understand and my parents couldn't intercede.

Instead, it will forever be a secret. One that I will carry alone.

Happy birthday to me.

This time it's my phone's ringing that brings me back to consciousness.

My window's curtain is shut firmly so I can't discern what time it is until my hand finally snatches the device off my bedside table. It's 11:14 PM.

I answer the call. "What?" I expel the word out harshly. I almost made it through my birthday without having to face the reality of it all.

"Sunday! It's time. I'm worried about you. It's your birthday! I'm outside, get dressed. You're coming with me." Carrie's bubbly voice slurs, and I have minimal interest to crawl out of the comfort of my bed.

If it were three weeks ago, before Tripp and Auggie's death, I wouldn't have even answered the phone. Carrie and I may be friends, but it is a friendship based out of obligation, not interests, from back when she dated my brother. Even so, I know Carrie is a kind-hearted person that means well. So, why not? I am already awake now and I can tell going back to sleep won't be an easy feat.

"Fine," I finally agree. Maybe this is what I need. To let loose, to try to forget, to further numb myself to the gaping holes that make up my heart.

I end the call and quickly get ready, throwing on shorts and a blouse from my laundry hamper. I don't have time for a shower, but I run a wet brush through my unruly copper curls and hope that it will be sufficient.

I find myself buzzing with energy. This is the first time I have done anything for *fun* since this all began. Will this even be enjoyable? I have my doubts. There is also a lump forming in my gut.

Guilt.

I promised Auggie years ago I would never go to one of these parties, especially not without him, but he isn't here now. And he isn't coming back. Maybe this will be the first step of going out on my own. Of living my life without the two men that took up so much space in it before.

I don't hear either of my parents as I exit my bedroom but that is to be expected. They both work in the hospital overnight, they won't be home for hours. I go to pull my bedroom door shut, but when I do, something catches my eye. My brother's room is next to mine and his door appears cracked open.

It shouldn't be.

"Sunday!!!" Carrie's yell comes from the front of my house.

Irritated and distracted, I shake my head and move my attention from Auggie's room. I promise myself I will investigate it later, and I head to the annoyingly drunk girl.

With Julia gone, she is my only remaining friend and the only person that remembered it was my birthday.

June 19th

"There you are!" Carrie pulls me into a tight hug as soon as I open the door, bouncing us up and down together.

It takes all of my willpower not to fall apart in her arms. I didn't realize it, but I needed a hug. I am craving human contact.

Behind her, I see a black BMW and curse. "You didn't tell me Maxwell was with you," I admonish Carrie, separating from her.

Carrie's newest boyfriend, Maxwell Thorne, is also one of the founding families of this town we all live in. He isn't old money, he is ancient money. Everything in this town can be traced back to the Thornes in one way or another.

What's more—Maxwell's best friend, William, is the sheriff's son. The two families together have their hands on anything and everything that goes on in this town. It's part of the reason so many leave after graduation and never return.

There's nothing exactly wrong with either of the guys, but something about both has always given me the heebie-jeebies. And combined with who their families are? Either could easily get away with murder.

Carrie's sharp fingernails digging into my wrist has me snapping back to her.

"Come on Sunday!!" she exclaims excitedly, not deterred by my annoyance. "Maxwell is sober and he's throwing a kegger at his house tonight.

It will be fun I promise. And if you hate it? Well, we can leave and find a good spot to watch the stars together."

My resolve softens. Carrie may seem like a typical ditsy blonde, but I know that she is one of the kindest women in existence. If I asked her to ditch her boyfriend, I know she would. But I don't want to do that to her.

"Okay," I agree. I try to follow her towards the car, but a hand snaps out from behind yanking me back by my blouse.

I go to scream, but another firm hand claps over my mouth.

"Stop it, I'm not going to hurt you." Axel's rough voice sends a thousand volts of electricity across my skin.

Carrie turns back to see why I have stopped my progress and her face goes white. "Axel," she acknowledges the man that has now removed his hand from my mouth.

He moves it to my stomach, holding me even more firmly in place. "We'll meet you at the party." Axel's words leave no room for argument.

But that's exactly what I want to do. I don't know Axel and I certainly don't want to listen to him.

He's a creepy asshole that basically jumped out of the bushes in the middle of the night and then began to dictate what I should or shouldn't do.

Except the warmth and strength of his grip is hard to ignore. Even more difficult are the parallels to his twin. But those similarities are only surface level. Tripp would never be this aggressive with me. Tripp was always a sweetheart.

Carrie's face appears unsure. I can't understand why Axel is here, but I don't want her to be any more involved than she needs to be. "I'll meet you there." I offer up the best reassuring smile I can.

I'm not sure if it's due to her noticeably drunken state, but she accepts the sudden change of events easily. She lifts her hand in mock salute and spares me only one more glance as she makes the rest of the way to the BMW that still idles on the road.

I watch her the entire way, ignoring the man at my back. When she opens the car door, I can just make out the shadowed face of Maxwell in the driver's seat, before she shuts the door and he peels away.

June 19th

I yank free of Axel's clutches and turn to him. "What do you want?" I refuse to meet his eyes and instead stare at a point above his shoulder.

"Happy birthday." His voice is smooth, liquid, as he shoves something into my hand.

I bring it up and examine the item.

Narcan.

What the fuck?

"Is this some kind of joke?" My words leave in a whisper. The wind kicks up and my curls wrap around us both in a shroud. I'm suddenly acutely aware I am on my front lawn in the middle of the night with a man that was convicted of a brutal assault.

With a man that looks exactly like Tripp.

I stare down at the Narcan. I've never done drugs.

Why would he be handing me this?

"Keep it with you, you're going to need this. Could save a life."

My skin prickles in apprehension, but I shake it off.

I scoff. "I don't do drugs," I say as I finally meet his bright eyes. They are a stark contrast to the dangerously dark man before me. A shiver rolls down my spine. "I'm not like you," I spit the words at him.

Axel smirks. His full lips flatten into a line, but it's not in anger. It's in exasperation. As if the notion *I don't need Narcan* is ridiculous.

"Look–" I pocket the item and put my hands up to allow space between us.

He catches my wrists, trapping me in place. I ignore the flurry of emotions that tumble through my belly. A million butterflies take hold, but it's not a good feeling. These butterflies are alive and they're trying to escape.

"What is wrong with you all? You lost your brother. I lost mine. Leave me to grieve in peace." I don't understand why he's out here, why he's trying to control what I do.

His already darkened face is now entirely void of light. Except his bright emerald eyes, they mock me.

They're an exact replica of Tripp's.

All of my previous annoyance leaves me and a sob wracks through my body. I squeeze my eyes shut as my vision blurs and my shoulders tremble.

None of this is fair.

Whatever Axel was expecting, it wasn't my tears, but still, he doesn't let me go. Instead, he pulls me to him and cradles me to his chest.

For a moment I permit myself to fall into his embrace. To imagine it isn't him at all, but a different man that used to comfort me exactly like this.

The charade doesn't last long. Axel isn't soft like Tripp was, he is all hard edges. The feel of his belt buckle pressing into my stomach is what snaps the dream, and I jump out of his arms.

"It's my birthday, I'm going to the party. I want to have *fun*." I don't owe him anything, not even this explanation, but I suspect he is going to attempt to stop me.

Axel's eyes scrunch up in annoyance, but he doesn't argue. "Fine," he finally states aggrievedly.

I turn to go. It's only a few miles and the walk will clear my mind from whatever this interaction was, but he once more reaches out to my blouse. Holding me in place.

"You can go. But you're coming with me. I'm meeting Darius there."

I open my mouth to firmly disagree.

"It wasn't a question, Sunday." My name is velvet leaving his lips. Had he ever said it before? I can't recall. He went to prison at the start of his junior year and we hadn't spent much time together prior.

His words finally catch up to my brain, but I don't have a chance to reply as he begins tugging me along to their house next door.

In their driveway sits a single vehicle. A motorcycle.

June 20th

"It's my birthday. Can you please just leave me be?"

Axel *tsks* and holds up his phone. It's 12:01 AM. "Get on." He lets go of his grip on me to yank the helmet off the handles. He tosses it at my chest.

I catch it just before it lands. "What is this?" I ask. I still don't understand why he is talking to me, why he is manhandling me.

"It's a helmet." Axel's condescending tone prickles my irritation.

"Fucking *obviously*."

He laughs. "Is the innocent Sunday cursing already?" Once more he's invading my space. He guides the helmet to my head and clips it under my chin. His fingers linger longer than needed and I savor the touch.

Savor the touch? Disgust shoots through me. He isn't Tripp. Tripp is dead. Axel is nothing like Tripp. Axel is sharp lines, emotional outbursts, darkness, and danger. The exact opposite of Tripp.

Whatever is on my face causes Axel's to turn into an impenetrable mask.

He puts a long leg over the bike and settles into the front. "Get on," he barks gruffly, gesturing behind him.

I'm not sure how I ended up in this moment tonight, but why not? He can drive me to the party, and then I can find Carrie and forget this entire interaction occurred. I don't know Axel, but he wouldn't try to hurt me. At least I don't think he would. There's definitely something off with the three brothers, but it doesn't seem... deadly.

I hope.

Decision made. I settle behind him on the seat, attempting to put as much space between us as possible.

"No, you're going to hold onto me and not let go. You fucking hear me? You let go and you'll tumble off." He reaches back and yanks me forward.

This close to him I can feel every muscle through the leather jacket he wears. I have done my best not to take in any of his appearance, but now I am forced to sculpt my body to his. It's worse than when he held me. I can't escape this.

Before I can change my mind and jump off the bike, he turns on the engine and jolts out the driveway.

His dark silky hair is just long enough to whip against the visor of the helmet. To avoid it, I push my face firmly against his back as best I can.

I hold on tight waiting for the ride to end. Ignoring how much I enjoy it. The warmth of his body, the smell of leather that sneaks into my helmet, the heart pumping adrenaline.

Auggie and Tripp, if only they could see me now.

They would both be furious.

After a short while, we come to a stop and Axel unpeels my arms that are secured around him.

I unstick my helmet from his jacket and take in my surroundings.

The party is in full swing, but thankfully Axel parks us on the outskirts of the chaos.

Axel gracefully untangles himself from the bike, but when I go to do the same, my foot catches and he's forced to catch my weight as I sprawl onto him. He doesn't even flinch, he simply grasps my hips with his large hands.

"Again?" Axel huffs the word as he places me back upright; it is oddly familiar. As if there is a memory of this somewhere deep in the recesses of my mind. Except I have never been on a motorcycle before.

Once Axel is satisfied, he lets go and removes my helmet.

I ignore the uneasy feeling, the heat of his fingers on my chin, his intense unfaltering attention and whip my head away as soon as he's done.

"Well, thanks?" My cheeks are flushed at this point from a mixture of embarrassment and irritation.

Axel chuckles softly. It's so similar in tone to Tripp that I flick my eyes back to him.

My vision blurs and it takes me a moment to realize I'm crying. I don't need to think any further into this entire interaction. Instead, I sprint off in the direction of the party, wiping my eyes furiously as I go.

Once again running away from an O'Brien.

June 20th

I make it all the way across the yard and through the front door before I finally find a familiar face.

"Carrie!" I yell her name through the crowd of partygoers. She is standing in the kitchen with a cup in her hand surrounded by half the football team. Among them are William and Maxwell, deep in conversation.

It takes some maneuvering, but I am able to finally make it to her side, albeit I am a sweating and trembling mess. This isn't an environment I am comfortable in, and it takes everything in me to not cover my ears at the drunken chaos in my vicinity.

"There you are!" When I am close enough, Carrie pulls me into a hug. She is unfortunately even more drunk than before, and her sudden movement has me scrambling to keep my balance.

"Easy now, don't hurt her." A set of hands on my shoulders pulls me back from Carrie. They lean me against the counter before their weight drops.

"Rayden," I acknowledge him gratefully. He's Maxwell's older brother, another Thorne, but unlike Maxwell, I don't mind his company. He was on the football team with my brother until he graduated two years ago. Instead of heading to college and never returning, like most everyone does, Rayden stayed here to work for his parents. I always respected that about him—even as loaded as his family is, he never takes it for granted. And while I guess that makes him technically a nepo baby, I don't judge him too much on it, he's always been nice to me and doesn't seem like a cocky asshole. Exactly the opposite of his brother.

"Well, hello there, Miss Sunday." Rayden flashes a smile, I think he means for it to be comforting, but it is all teeth.

"Sorry about that Sunday, I think I may have had too much. Here." Carrie pushes her full cup of mystery liquid into my hands. I take it without thinking.

"I need to go to the bathroom, watch her for me, will you?" she directs that last part to Rayden.

I try to protest, but she's already stumbling across the room and while I don't especially like Maxwell, I am grateful when he breaks off the conversation he's in and helps guide her away.

I know that drinking something I didn't watch get poured is not the best idea, but at this moment, with my anxiety riding me, I don't care. I gulp down the liquid, ignoring the burn as it settles uneasily in my empty stomach.

"Easy there." Rayden gently pulls the drink back from my mouth.

A single drop escapes my lips and rolls down my chin. Before I can wipe it away, Rayden's sleeve is swiping across my face.

Rayden smiles again, and this time, it isn't as off-putting as it spreads to his soft chocolate eyes before hardening a bit. "How have you been?" Rayden is leaning down into my space now, the question a caress against my ear.

I stiffen at both his proximity and the words. "Can we not do this? *Please?*" I whisper the last word out as it cracks. I am here to forget, not be pitied and reminded of how horrible the rest of my life is going to be without my brother. Without Tripp.

Something flashes across Rayden's eyes as he stands back up to his full height, but then he places a new drink in my hand. This time it is an unopened beer. "Fair enough. For what it's worth, I miss him too."

Guilt squirms its way up my throat. "I'm sorry, I didn't mean to—" I begin to apologize. Of course, I am not the only one hurting.

"Think nothing of it," Rayden laughs caustically. "Drink that instead though, I did promise to always keep an eye on you, and I know you aren't exactly the drinking type."

His thoughtfulness does nothing to appease my inner turmoil. "Thank you," I murmur softly. He's right, whatever I chugged is already working its way through my system, but I find myself enjoying the numbness it brings.

Once more an emotion flickers across Rayden's face that I can't discern, but before I can think too much more into it, William joins our bubble.

"Never thought I would see the day that Sunday the nun would bum it with us at a house party. I thought you were too good for this?" William's voice is mocking, and his icy eyes are a mirror of his tone.

"Knock it off man." Rayden shoulder checks William, but the words have already landed in my gut. They mix with the alcohol, blending uneasily. Nausea bubbles up.

I want to make my escape, but yet another person joins our group. "Sunday," the sweet voice greets me, "is my brother giving you any trouble?" It's Veronica, Auggie's most recent girlfriend and William's older sister.

I meet her kind, soft eyes and find myself noticeably relaxing. "Hi Veronica, it's good to see you, sorry it's been so long."

Understanding and empathy creep across her face. Veronica has always been a kind girl. My brother agreed with this sentiment and that's why they had been dating for the last year in college. I hadn't really spent too much time around her though.

"Are you–" I am not quite sure how to articulate the question "–are you doing okay?" I finally settle on the words, and even to my ears, they sound flat.

Veronica's mask wavers a bit, but then she slides it back into place. "You two? Give us some space." She pushes both the men away and I realize we are now the only ones remaining in the kitchen. In fact, as I look around, judging by the stomping above and the distant DJ music, most of the party has moved outside or upstairs.

Rayden offers up one more reassuring smile before dragging William away with him.

Once the men are a distance from us, Veronica hops on the counter and gestures for me to join her. It takes a few attempts, but eventually I am seated next to her. Our knees are touching and we are facing each other as best we can.

A random thought strikes. "Have you seen Tiffany?" Tiffany was Maxwell's last girlfriend, a cheerleader. She isn't at the party which, from what I heard, isn't the norm. I want to talk to her, see if Carrie is going to be okay with him.

I finally look up and see that Veronica is ashen. "Didn't you hear? She got a full ride scholarship and said she wouldn't be coming back here," she finally says matter-of-factly. The words don't match her expression... at all. Her tone is reassuring, but her gaze is flickering around, eyebrows knitted in concern, lips drawing into a line.

That's odd... but I don't get a chance to push the matter.

"I figured you might need to vent, and maybe I do too if that's okay?" Veronica redirects, her voice softening.

My uneasiness thaws into empathy and I accept the pivot. I know all too well what it is like to lose a first love, and from what I heard, my brother was hers.

"Yes." I had set down the beer in order to get up here, but I find myself grabbing it again. Opening the tab, I take a long sip.

Veronica gives me a sad, wistful look, sighing softly. "You know I was supposed to go with them? The only reason I didn't was because Will made me come home the night before. It's why I couldn't make it to their memorial. It was too much, I am sorry." Veronica reaches out, squeezing my hand.

A chill rolls down my spine and I don't know what to say. She essentially cheated death, what if William hadn't done that?

"Wow." I know the shock is clear across my face, making up for my lack of response. The rest of her words process through. "You don't need to apologize for not being there, I understand. I almost wish I didn't go either." My mind flashes back to the lightning strike and my interaction with the remaining O'Briens.

"Thanks, Sunday. I appreciate your understanding." Veronica drops my hand and looks in the direction of her brother. "But, yeah, I think that might be why Will is being an extra asshole, he knows how close he came to losing me too," Veronica states, shrugging a shoulder. "Not that the circumstance gives him any excuse to talk to you the way he did."

"You heard that?" I grimace. "He's not wrong though, if *that* hadn't happened, I most likely wouldn't be here."

"Look, I know we never really hung out before, but I have always liked you and your brother thought the world of you." Veronica gives a sad laugh. "It's okay to not want to party, it's not for everyone. But since you are new to this, just be careful, okay?"

"I will."

"Also, if anything gets too tough I want you to call or text me. Is it alright if I do too? I feel like there isn't anyone that I can really talk to about this."

Veronica pulls a phone out of her dress pocket. She hands me the device and gestures for me to do the same.

Unlocking it, I hand it to her, she raises a questioning eyebrow.

"Axel's number?" she asks worriedly. "Why do you have his number?"

I choke on the sip of beer I was in the process of swallowing. "What, I don't?"

She turns my phone to me, and sure enough there it is. That sneaky asshole must have added his number when he took it earlier. "Be careful with him. You know what happened, don't you?" Her eyebrows are furrowed together.

For some unknown reason, I am suddenly feeling extremely defensive of Axel. I knew he went to prison, but it was over kicking the ass of one of Maxwell's friends, Mark. I have a hard time believing Mark didn't deserve it. But I don't want to explain all of that when Veronica is just trying to be nice and watch out for me.

"I will," I agree, exchanging our phones back. I am not sure if I will take Veronica's offer, but it warms my heart to know that there is at least someone else I could talk to. Or maybe that is just the buzz of alcohol that is steadily creeping up on me.

Veronica goes to hop off the counter, but stops. She squeezes my shoulder softly. "Please reach out if you need me?"

I smile at her, my first real smile in what feels like a lifetime. "I will."

Her face softens. "Oh, and I wasn't sure if I should ask you, but did you like your graduation gift?"

The question has me stuttering, *graduation gift?*

"What? What do you mean?" I ask, confused.

Veronica's eyes glass over. "Oh, shit, I'm sorry. It must have been in the car, when they—when he—" A sob wracks through her body and I find myself leaning forward as best I can to wrap her in my arms.

I realize in that moment, maybe Veronica needs me just as much as I need her. "I'll find it." I promise. She is shaking in my arms, and I discover that comforting her is making me feel stronger. As if I, too, can get through this. "You know, I am here too if you need me."

Veronica pulls away from me, water streaks down her cheeks, but she offers up a kind smile. "I may just take you up on that."

June 20th

I need to use the bathroom. Veronica headed outside a minute ago, and I promised I would follow her, right after I relieved myself.

Which I am about to do in this swanky bedroom if I can't find a bathroom soon. This is a certified mansion and I am questioning whose bright idea it was not to have more bathrooms.

Exiting the bedroom, I hear someone calling me.

"Sunday." The last voice I want to hear is only a few feet away, but maybe he will help me.

"William," I acknowledge.

William's eyes are glassy and he shifts unsteadily from foot to foot. He has clearly drank more since I saw him last and, even in my own hindered state, it makes my hackles rise.

"Can you please point me in the direction of the bathroom?" I decide on the high road. Maybe William is just hurting, maybe he is working through the fact that he nearly lost his sister.

His finger points to a door; it's the only one I hadn't tried. Of course.

I spin away and rush to the bathroom, do my business, and hope he will be gone when I exit. At this point the alcohol has done its job, and I am feeling *better*. Well not exactly better but less bothered. As if the world will not, in fact, destroy me.

I give myself one cursory glance in the mirror as I wash my hands. The pale face and sunken cheekbones are new, but my eyes are just as dull as usual. Tripp said they were reminiscent of a galaxy, but all I see is a storm. The dark blue hues almost blacken in the dimmed light of the bathroom.

When I exit, William is still standing there. I go to walk around him, but he catches my arm. "Nuh-uh, if you are going to come to a party, you are going to hang out with the adults."

William is not hurting; he is just a certified asshole.

I test his grip and decide not to fight yet. William is a jerk, but his sister likes me. That should be enough for him to not harm me, right? I am not sure if it is the alcohol or my own stupidity, but I don't struggle as he yanks me to the stairs. Even when he drags me up them instead of down.

My fear doesn't truly ignite until he pushes me into a room.

I know for a fact I have never been in it, but it is eerily familiar.

"Sunday School..." Maxwell sits on a large bed, a tray in his hand. "I see you found her?" he addresses to the man still trapping my arm.

"As requested," William grunts, pushing me forward.

I catch my balance before stumbling entirely onto Maxwell.

"Easy there." Maxwell sets the tray down and his hands lift to my waist steadying me. He yanks me a bit until I am standing between his thighs. I attempt to escape his hold, all it does is cause his fingers to crush into my hip bones.

"Where's Carrie?" I ask anxiously, looking around as if she is hiding in the room and is going to pop out and tell me this is a sick joke. Except she isn't here. This isn't right. I shouldn't be in this bedroom with these two men. They are dangerous.

A lump forms in my throat and I find it incredibly hard to swallow, difficult to breathe. A sheen of sweat forms on my palms, I don't even have the space to wipe them on my shorts. That is how close Maxwell is to me.

A soft smile graces Maxwell's face, it doesn't reach his eyes. "Sleeping." His fingers are cattle prods, burning into my bones as he refuses to let me budge even an inch.

I am not drunk enough to ignore that I am scared. Terrified. I want to scream, but would that even help?

William steps up behind me, breathing down my neck. "What happened to the tough girl downstairs? Girls like you shouldn't be here." The threat rolls down my spine.

"Then, I'll just be going." I try to escape their embrace, but I am surrounded. My nerves are buzzing with energy, willing me to do something.

But what can I do?

Maxwell looks over my shoulder at William before dropping his hands and pouring something onto the tray.

I go to step back, but William won't allow me to budge more than an inch and now it is his arms wrapping around my waist, holding me captive.

"Initiation." Maxwell lifts the tray to me, a rolled-up bill between two of his fingers.

The white line stares up at me. I have never done drugs, but I'm not an idiot, I know what they look like.

"Will you let me go if I do this?" I am not sure which of the men I am asking.

"Of course," William agrees, but I can't help but notice the darkness that swallows Maxwell's face.

I want to just do it, get it over with, but when I lean forward to take the bill, the Narcan in my pocket presses against Maxwell's thigh. I know enough about drugs to also know what fentanyl is. This looks like it's cocaine, but what else is in there? What if the first time I try drugs, it kills me?

I pause.

Maxwell doesn't like that.

"Too fucking good for us, aren't you little Sunday School? Just a little nun out in the world alone. No more big brother to keep her safe." His hateful words land exactly how he wishes them to. "If you don't want the line, I have something else you can have, church girl."

I don't like what I see in Maxwell's eyes, he isn't going to let this go. How far will he take this? I'm internally panicking. My heart's beat is painful, my stomach is one large painful knot, my head is throbbing. I don't know what to do. Maxwell is right–in the past, if I got myself into a sticky situation, Auggie was always there to bail me out.

In the moment of silence where I am just soaking in the pain and terror. I hear it.

Boots are thundering outside the room.

"Help!" I manage to get the word out before William slaps a hand over my mouth.

The three of us pause, listening for the steps. After a few moments pass of nothing, I realize I may not escape this unscathed, but then there is a loud crashing noise behind me.

The door. It's the door crashing open.

"Get the fuck off her. Don't make me kick your asses, too." Axel's threat has William dropping his hold on me.

Before I can move to escape, Maxwell jerks a hand out catching on the hem of my shorts. "Better watch yourself." He drops his hold and pushes me back just as Axel makes it to me.

Axel grabs my hand and leads me angrily out of the room. He doesn't stop his stomping until we are down the two flights of stairs and out the backdoor.

When we make it outside, I see that Darius is leaning against a dark car.

Ten feet away from Darius, he finally stops and grabs me by the shoulders staring down at me. "Do you have any idea how stupid that was? What they could have done to you? Did you do any fucking drugs?"

I don't expect the venom he spits at me, but I deserve it. I let my hair fall in a curtain around my face as I begin to cry. The terror is still swirling against my skin and it's only the hold Axel has on me that keeps me leveled in reality.

He shakes me. "Answer my fucking questions!" This time his words are dripping with an unknown inflection, but it is almost reminiscent of concern.

"Ease up, man." Darius's gentle tone is what pulls me out of my head.

Axel lets go of me. "Get the answers" is all he says before he storms away.

I didn't even thank him. My sobs intensify. I am useless and stupid and nothing I do is ever right.

My brother is dead.

Their brother is dead.

And it's all my fault.

"Shhh." Darius hauls me into his arms and pats my back softly. "It's going to be okay, but I need you to tell me. Did you do anything they gave you?"

"No," I hiccup out. How did Axel even know about that? He was in the room for all of five seconds before yanking me away. Was this normal for Maxwell?

"That's good," Darius continues, offering soft affirmations as his hand circles a path on my back soothingly.

His voice is so incredibly comforting, it isn't long before my sobs lessen and all that is left are annoying hiccups. I wipe my face as best I can, but the muggy summer air has my hair sticking to my neck and I realize how incredibly uncomfortable I am. I just want to curl up in my bed and forget any of this ever happened.

"Come on, ride home with us?" he asks it as if it's a question, but he is already leading me to the car.

I keep my eyes firmly on my shoes as we walk. He opens the back door and guides me gently into the seat. He leans over and grabs hold of the seatbelt, extending it across me and clicks it in place.

My eyes meet his as he lingers there, just staring at me. I can see the sadness coating Darius, I can feel that he wants to say something else, but the sound of arguing outside has him jerking back. He hits his head on the inside of the car because the shift is so abrupt, and we both wince at the impact.

"I'll be right back." Darius offers up a reassuring smile that doesn't quite meet his golden eyes before shutting the car door.

I move my attention to outside, and I find that the arguing is between Grayson and Axel.

I watch as Darius approaches them. Most of their words are inaudible but some are raised just loud enough for me to catch.

"She was in a new room—" Axel's voice is coated in anger.

"Did she—" Grayson is cut off by Darius's approach.

Darius shakes his head.

"Out of our sight—" Axel's voice lowers, and I have a hard time making out the rest, but they all turn their attention towards me.

"I'll talk to them," Grayson grumbles out in warning, and I see him walk towards me through the car window.

He wrenches open the driver's door and slams it shut, he takes a few steadying breaths before turning to me. "You okay?" His tone is jarring. His voice is a combination of sugar and spice.

I don't have a chance to answer as Darius pulls the back door open on the other side of me.

He slides in until we are touching. Leg to leg. Shoulder to arm. Knee to thigh. I didn't realize how much larger Darius is than me, but this close together it's hard to miss.

I know I shouldn't be allowing this, but I need comfort. I am not sure if it is the shock or the alcohol or something else in-between, but I feel raw. Like at the most minor inconvenience, I will lose the rest of my marbles.

"Axel is going to take his bike back. Cool his head," Darius advises us. He lifts his arm and wraps it around my shoulders pulling me further into his comfort.

I watch Grayson's face shimmer in the rearview mirror, but he says nothing.

I burrow firmly into Darius and allow myself this small moment of comfort. I find the solace that I didn't realize I so desperately needed. I do my best to ignore the guilt hammering its way down my throat, reminding me that I am the reason their brother drove home. That he would have had no motive to if not for me. I am the cause of why they were out on the roads during that storm, why their car hydroplaned off the road.

"I'm sorry. For everything," I whisper softly into Darius's cotton shirt. His warmth and smoky smell envelop me and it's not long before I lose myself to unconsciousness.

But before I do, I swear I hear him say, "None of this is your fault."

June 20th

My mouth is dry, tastes disgusting, and my head is pounding to a drummer's beat. Ugh. Those are my first thoughts as I wake up.

How did I get here? Is shortly after.

I am back in my bedroom, but I have no recollection of *how*. The last thing I remember is the party.

The party.

Maxwell. William. The room, the drugs, and then Axel.

Grayson driving us. Darius's comfort and warmth.

My cheeks heat in embarrassment. What was I thinking?

I have no clue what time it is, my bedroom is shrouded in darkness but that means nothing with my curtains currently drawn. I reach out a hand and find my phone. It's on the charger. 12:05 PM.

I expect the texts from both Veronica and Carrie. It's the one from Axel that I don't, he sent it around an hour ago.

You have a few hours. Get packed.

What the fuck does that mean?

Banging on my door distracts me from the cryptic message.

"Sunday, get dressed and come downstairs. We need to talk." My mother's voice is toneless, teetering on exhausted.

This isn't going to be good. I shoot texts to Veronica and Carrie. The one to Carrie is challenging because what exactly should I tell her about

Maxwell? Would she even believe me? I'm beginning to suspect his last girlfriend, Tiffany, left this town to get away from him.

I allow myself a few more moments of peace before pushing up from my bed. I blink as I spot something. Next to where my phone sits is a red velvet cupcake—my favorite—wrapped in plastic. On top of it is a note.

Happy Birthday

My parents must have left it. Happiness flushes my system; I didn't realize how much it hurt that my parents hadn't wished me a happy birthday. I know they have been just as overwhelmed as me, but forgetting my birthday? Well, it hurt.

Exiting the bed with a bit more enthusiasm now, I take a short period to refresh and get dressed.

When I leave and go to shut my door behind me, I instinctively look to Auggie's room. The door is sealed firmly now. Odd, I could have sworn yesterday that it was left open.

Another memory pierces me: my graduation present, the one Victoria mentioned at the party last night.

They returned the items in his pockets but nothing from the car, not even his phone. What if it is just sitting there, in the vehicle? I shake the thought away, first I need to talk to my mom then I can go into detective mode.

The sight that greets me in our dining room has my anxiety boiling over.

Both of my parents are sitting at the table but so is Grayson.

What the actual fuck.

My mom gestures for me to sit. The Narcan Axel gave me the night before sits on the table in front of them.

A beacon of betrayal. I have never done drugs, why would they give that to my parents? Other than to paint me in a bad light.

What the fuck?

I pull the chair out slowly, dragging it against the hardwood floor, and try my best to discern what in the ever-loving fuck is going on. From the look on all three of their faces, it isn't good.

"Sunflower," my mom starts, the nickname has me even more on guard, she uses it only when relaying bad news. Pain pierces my heart, the nickname is one Auggie gave me and, even worse, the last time she used it, I was learning of Tripp and Auggie's deaths. "I know this hasn't been easy for you, for any of us."

My eyes flash to Grayson, he refuses to make contact. Looking pointedly above my head. "Yes," I agree. Because of course it isn't easy. They lost their favorite and I lost two people that truly cared about me.

"We forgot your birthday, sweetie." This time it's my dad's rough voice that pulls my attention.

"The cupcake?" I ask.

Confusion ripples across both of their faces, but Grayson's is coated in understanding. "Darius," he states.

Something bubbles up in my gut. A mixture of anger and guilt. Of happiness and misery. "Oh," I expel the word.

It hurts more than I expected it to, that neither of my parents remember me in the absence of their son. I don't blame them; my brother was larger than life. He casts a shadow even in death.

"Sunflower, we were already planning this," she pauses, "before everything *happened* we were assigned travel contracts. We thought it would be okay to leave you here alone, but after what Grayson told us, and what we found, we think it is best that you stay under his roof. Grayson has been an upstanding man over the years doing his best to watch over his family, he's even helping Axel get his life back on track. He can keep watch over you, so you stay out of trouble."

I fall back in my chair. The text suddenly makes sense. *Get packed.* Axel knew, but why would they want me there? Besides the memorial and the party last night, we haven't ever exactly been close. But here is Grayson, sitting in my dining room. Telling my mother whatever he did to have her concerned. He may have lived next to me all my life, but he was Auggie's friend, not mine.

"I can take care of myself here." The words sound flat even to me.

"Sweetie," my dad says, brushing his curly hair from his eyes. They're sunken in. Listless. "We don't want you to be alone. We need to have someone to look out for you. We trust Grayson, he is a good man, he will keep you safe. And if you need anything you can always call us, too. The other option is we can send you to your grandmother's."

Why do they have so much trust in Grayson? And absolutely not, my grandmother lives on a farm in the middle of nowhere. She doesn't even have internet or anything except animals. If I feel lonely now, it won't be anything compared to out there. "I'm eighteen," I try again.

"Sunflower, you don't even have a job. Next year you'll go off to college, but you made the decision to stay here, to take a gap year, and if we are supporting you financially that means you will abide by our rules. Grayson was kind enough to offer to watch over you, don't disrespect him by being ungrateful." Her voice is final. There will not be a way out of this.

My fight leaves my body and I deflate further into the chair. "Okay," I huff out. Grayson finally tries to meet my eyes, but it's my turn to look pointedly away.

He sold me out.

"When?" I ask.

"Today, in the next couple of hours. Go pack up what you'll need, we will be back as soon as we can to check on you, sweetie." My dad's gentle tone does nothing to soothe the stifling dread.

I am used to them committing most of their time to their jobs, but I never expected they would leave me just weeks after my brother died. Before more emotion can well up, I jerk back from the table and stomp towards my bedroom.

I can hear Grayson and my parents discussing the details of my new home. They're promising to pay him, and tell him that if I am too much, they can ship me off to my grandmother's, that they'll answer if he ever needs to call. As if I am a dog they are putting up in an animal hotel.

I push down my simmering anger as I approach my bedroom. Before I enter, though, I decide to go into Auggie's. Maybe my gift somehow made it back there? Maybe he had it delivered here?

When I push into his bedroom, I don't expect the crippling pressure of sadness to weigh my feet down, but I persevere and shut the door softly behind me.

His room isn't right. It's too clean. As if someone had tidied up every mess he left behind. Did our mom do this? When Auggie went to college, he left his room in chaos, and I teased him about it.

It's almost as if every trace of him is already disappearing. For the hundredth time since I heard of his death, I am sobbing. Stepping to the bed, I fall onto it. It still smells like him, like the sheets weren't cleaned, the bed was just made. Why would our mom do this?

His oak desk sits within arm's reach of the bed and I find myself extending my arm behind it. We have a matching pair, except mine is painted teal. There's a spot on the backside of the drawer that he used to hide anything he didn't want our parents to find. He finally told me about it when I was in high school.

Sunflower, you better not tell our parents, but if there's ever anything you need to hide, put it behind your desk, one of the drawers has a false back.

I smile at the memory as I find my way and pop the back open. Feeling something, I sit up to get a better look.

There are only two items. A flip phone and a picture.

I have just a moment to look at the picture before a noise outside the room has me jerking them into my pocket, just in time for Grayson to open the door.

My heart is pounding loudly in my ears. I am in shock from what I just saw, but I don't have time to question why my brother had a burner phone, why he had a picture of a girl, why in the picture it looks like an unknown man is attempting to assault her.

Grayson is frowning. "Find something?"

I do my best to calm my nerves, to not show my emotions. "No," I mutter out, lifting off the bed. As I do, I reach back on my brother's pillows and grab his stuffed giraffe. It smells like him.

I try to walk past Grayson, but he steps into the room and shuts the door behind him. Unlike with William, there is no terror, just annoyance. And a very odd distant sense of déjà vu. It's just a feeling, but I can't shake it.

Why am I instinctually comfortable with Grayson, Darius, and even Axel? I trust them more than I should.

"What do you want?" Once again anger shoots out from a dark depth inside me.

Grayson's face is almost apologetic, but I don't want to hear it.

I push on his chest. He doesn't budge. Instead, he captures my wrist. His grip is gentle, careful, delicate. Even still, where he binds me leaves a fire in its wake. My other hand holds the giraffe as a barrier between us as he keeps me there.

"You may not understand now, but I did this for you. I am just trying to watch out for you," he growls the words into the top of my hair.

"You don't even know me! None of you do!" I snark the words out frustratedly. I want to scream the words, but I don't want my parents to come in here. For them to shame me for being *ungrateful*.

"You're wrong" is all Grayson says, before dropping my wrist and allowing me to pass. "Your parents want you to be ready to leave in the next thirty minutes. I'll be waiting."

I expect him to follow me when I leave Auggie's room, but he doesn't.

Once more I am confused by an O'Brien brother. How could he possibly know me? Why is he so gung-ho on infiltrating my life? And why did he seem to know I found something in my brothers' room?

The items weigh heavily in my pocket as I begin to pack up my life. I don't have time to investigate now.

But I have a plan in mind and the first step is to search his car, even if it breaks me to see the place where they both died.

Auggie, I wish you were here. I need you.

June 20th

This day is dragging on forever.

My suitcase bumps behind me down the sidewalk, the sun blazing down and causing my hair to stick to my neck. Grayson left before I did to allow *heartfelt* goodbyes with my parents.

They both patted me awkwardly on the shoulder and told me to stay out of trouble.

It's hard to be angry with either of them. They were never bad parents. They did what they could to raise us. I was never hungry, never lacking in anything, except maybe their attention. But that seems to be the norm in modern society where both parents have to work overtime to make ends meet. Especially with a two-child household. I'm just mostly disappointed because, as much as I know I am alone with Auggie and Tripp gone, their actions have solidified the feeling.

Except I'm not alone. Physically at least. I am about to be surrounded by the remaining O'Brien brothers.

I push through the anxiety and approach the front door. It swings open before I can knock, and I am looking up at the youngest brother.

He graces me with a soft, apologetic smile. "I know this isn't what you want, but I promise it's for the best."

Darius isn't the one that sold me out to my parents, he hasn't earned my wrath. In fact... "Thank you for the cupcake, it's my favorite flavor." I ate the entire thing in three bites, but I don't relay that information. "And for last night." My cheeks blaze, it's not from the heat.

A gentle, knowing look shifts across his face. "I aim to please. Come on in, we have you in our mom's room."

I'm immensely grateful. Part of me was terrified they would put me in Tripp's room.

Stepping into the house, the AC hits me in a blast, and my sweat turns to a cold sheen as I take in the surroundings. I haven't been in this house except when I snuck in through Tripp's window.

I'm happily surprised by the cleanliness and warmth. It feels comfortable, lived in, and obviously well taken care of.

"Here." Darius gently takes my suitcase from me and begins leading the way.

I follow carefully behind, on the lookout for the other two brothers. My eyes perusing the walls. A picture of Tripp has me jerking to a stop. His arms are around Axel's shoulder. I can't exactly explain how I know which is which because they're both young boys in the image that look identical, but I inherently know that Tripp is the one on the left. He's smiling at the camera, while the other boy is frowning and appears to be bouncing out of his skin trying to stay still.

"So young," I whisper.

Darius turns back, sees what I am looking at, and pauses. "They were," he agrees. His attention catches on my fingers tracing the smiling boy. He opens his mouth as if to add more but shuts it, shaking his head.

My fingers unconsciously stroke Tripp's face. "I miss him." I'm not sure what compels me to speak the words, but here with Darius, I don't feel so alone. I don't feel like I need to carry my secrets.

"I know," Darius responds softly. His eyes are closed and he whips back around so quickly—leading the way—that I almost question if he spoke at all.

As we make it up a flight of stairs and to the door at the very end of the hallway, we pass Tripp's room and I can't help but allow my gaze to linger. Water wells up in my eyes again.

"Home sweet home." Darius pushes the door open at the very end, and I am surprised to see that the room looks incredibly comfortable and nice.

The bed is neatly made and covered in soft colorful pillows. There is also a dresser, desk, and TV that all look brand new. So new in fact that the plastic protector still covers the TV's screen. I had never been in their mom's room before, but I doubt she had it this carefully set up, doubt she bought furniture recently and just left it behind. From the few times I met her in passing, she was the epitome of chaos.

Foreboding flashes in my subconscious, threatening to take hold. Just like at the memorial, I recognize the feeling: *apprehension.*

Ever since the memorial I have had this inexplicable sensation. As if something bad is about to happen. As if there are memories pressing against my brain that aren't my own, and for some reason the feeling is always exacerbated when I am around the O'Briens.

Darius clearly sees something shift in my body language. He turns in the door and gestures around the space. "Our grandmother taught us to always be prepared for guests," he explains. He places my suitcase just inside the door and steps back allowing me to squeeze by his bulky frame into the room. "Make yourself comfortable, bathroom is through that door. Dinner should be ready around seven when Grayson and Axel get back, but if you're hungry before then feel free to make something. The fridge stays stocked."

My heart softens. They lost their grandmother not too long ago and now their brother, too. He is just trying to make me feel relaxed; he knows what I am going through. Because he is going through very close to the same thing.

I sit carefully on the bed and meet Darius's amber eyes. Darius again seems like he wants to say something, but he pauses as if re-thinking. "I know this isn't what you want, and nothing seems like it makes sense, but I promise we just want to do right by your brother. And you may not realize it, but Sunday, we do care about you."

"But you don't even know me." I realize how harsh the words are as soon as I say them, but I can't help it. This is so incredibly confusing, and they haven't really told me anything. They just keep showing up. Pushing their way into my life. Albeit thankfully so when it came to Maxwell and William.

"Don't we?" On that cryptic note, Darius turns and leaves me to my own devices.

I'm tired of all three of these brothers.

Tripp, if only you could see me now.

June 21st

My alarm blaring at 12:00 AM startles me awake. Right on time. I shut it off as quickly as possible. I have managed to avoid the brothers thus far, even going so far as to skip dinner.

But I woke up for a specific reason; I am going to sneak out, go to the police station, and demand my brother's items. I am so focused on my plan for tonight, that it takes me longer than it should to realize I'm not alone.

"*Sunday.*" An admonishing voice cuts through the room's darkness.

I jump in the bed. Using my phone's light, I locate the source. Axel is seated on the end of my bed, a knowing look gracing his features. I'm not sure if it's my freshly woken state, or the lighting, but he looks so much like Tripp in this moment that I choke on my next breath.

"What exactly do you have planned at this hour?" His lips lift cruelly, knowingly.

The mirage vanishes. *Axel.* I reach over to the lamp beside me, clicking it on. I am acutely aware that this is the monster under my bed I was always warned of. Except all the light does is cast him in eerie shadows, it does nothing to dispel him.

I blink a few more times. "Why are you here?" The question leaves my lips softer than I intend.

Axel's gaze openly peruses my body, slowly navigates my form. Until settling on my chest. He licks his lips.

My nipples pebble in the silky white shirt I fell asleep in. I suddenly feel on fire, the weight of his attention is causing me to combust and I need a reprieve. I open my mouth to tell him to leave, but he jumps forward before any words escape.

He pins me to the bed, my arms above my head, his hips pressed into mine.

His chest pushes into my sensitive nipples and I let out an accidental moan.

"Fuck!" he expels the word. "This is earlier than last time, but the hundredth time is the charm," he says before his head is bending to mine, his mouth capturing mine. His soft lips are unexpected compared to his hard, chiseled form. His body pushes me further down as his mouth claims mine. The passion and deep sadness in the kiss are unmistakable.

I want to blame my sleep deprived state, my endless grief, my need for comfort. But I can't. In this moment with Axel pressing me firmly into the mattress claiming my lips. Heating my body. Controlling my movements. I begin to come undone. When his tongue slips into my mouth, fighting mine, I allow myself to fall into the feelings.

My backup alarm has us both jumping apart.

Axel propels himself off the bed as if burned. I turn the alarm off, again. My lips are throbbing, desire is coursing throughout my body, but most of all...

My guilt.

What the fuck did I just allow him to do? Why did it feel so comfortable?

Because he reminds me of Tripp. The thought is jarring and accompanied by the familiar sting of tears.

When I finally gain the courage to, I meet Axel's gaze.

He is an impenetrable mask. "Whatever you were planning on doing tonight, don't do it. It's not worth it."

My earlier guilt is driven out as my anger peaks. How dare he! How dare he tell me what to do! How dare he invade my space! How dare he *kiss* me! "Who are you to tell me what to do?!" The words come out as a hushed scream.

Axel steps forward to the bed and bends down so he is inches from my face, for a moment I think he is going to kiss me again, but instead he smiles snidely. "Little girl. You have no idea what you are doing. You can't play with monsters unless you're willing to become one yourself." This time when he looks me up and down, it is mockingly. "And all I see in this bed is a Little Lamb." I try to turn my head away, but he catches my face, his calloused fingers gripping my cheeks. Tightly. He leans until his voice is directly in my ear. "Now listen, Little Lamb, I may not be a monster, but for you? I will wear its skin."

The hot air from his breath tickles my ear and causes me to shudder. Before I can even begin to unpack how I am feeling or what he is saying, Axel drops his grasp on me and leaves the room.

He turns back right before shutting the door behind him. His large size takes up the entire doorframe, his dark hair a ruffled mess, his sharp eyes swirling in chaos. In this light he looks exactly like the monster he promises to be. "You think you know who I am? But you have no fucking clue."

My heart pounds in my chest. I can hardly breathe. I need to get out of here. Out of my head. Axel's words echo around my brain. Why is everything these brothers say so confusing? And how did I allow him to kiss me? How did I permit myself to enjoy it as much as I did?

I won't be able to go back to sleep like this. My eyes catch on the window. More specifically, the stars shining through it. My plans will have to wait until tomorrow.

I step out of the bed on wobbly legs, allowing a moment for them to steady, before I head to the window, pushing up the frame.

Success.

There is a place to step out on; I should be able to do this. I lift out and up and climb very carefully until I reach my intended destination.

Finally on the roof, I lie back carefully and simply watch the stars. I allow myself a moment of peace, forgiveness, and reprieve.

It has been exactly twenty days on this planet without Tripp and Auggie. How long will I feel this soul sucking emptiness? Will I always walk around with two heavy plates in my heart? With the crippling guilt that anything I do would hurt the two? My fingers drift to my lips and I feel that they are still swollen.

How dare I kiss Axel? I can't believe I allowed myself to get caught in whatever that was. I am a horrible person and it's not even Axel's fault. He didn't know my connection to Tripp. To his twin.

Tripp and I kept our relationship hidden from our families. We knew if they found out it would only cause unwanted drama.

Fuck.

I focus on the stars in an attempt to quell my racing heart and it must work, because I don't even remember falling asleep.

I am not sure how I got there, but when I wake up, I'm back in their mom's room. I guess it's mine now.

This time, fully rested, I have formulated a more solid plan.

Calling Veronica, I get dressed as the phone rings. "Hey Sunday." Her voice is coated in sleep.

"Hey sorry, didn't mean to wake you. I just had a couple questions." I lock my bedroom door and find my suitcase. Locating the giraffe, I use my fingers to undo the zipper on the back and pull out the picture and flip phone. The phone is dead, and the charger type is something I don't have.

"Of course. You can call me anytime." Veronica's tone is a bit more steady now and her words swell in my chest. She was always good to my brother and I know first-hand the pain of tragically losing your first love.

I weigh my options. Would she know about these items? Auggie was last home only a month ago and he could have left them then. I start with the easier question. "You said Auggie got me a graduation present? Do you know what it would have looked like?"

"Yes," she murmurs softly. "It would have just been in an envelope. I hope you can find it."

I hope so too, and I know just where I am going to start my search. "Do you... do you know what happened to the car?"

Her breath hitches. "My guess would be the impound lot, but Sunday, I doubt it's there. The insurance company probably took it."

The words don't feel right, but I can tell she's crying now. I don't want to question her.

"I'm sorry Sunday, is it okay if I text you later? I didn't realize how hard this would be. You just—" she pauses "—you talk exactly like him, you know?"

My heart sinks. I didn't even think about that. But I understand. "I get it. You don't have to apologize, I appreciate you. And if you need someone to talk to, you can always reach out to me too." I realize, once again, that I may not be the only person feeling incredibly alone right now. I trace the picture with my finger.

Veronica hiccups. "I really appreciate that Sunday. I'll talk to you soon, promise."

While some of my questions have been answered, there is still one weighing heavily.

Why does my brother have this picture?

I don't recognize the girl that is laid flat on a bare bed, but she is clearly not conscious.

The angle of the picture makes it so the man on top of her takes up the remaining frame, but it's just the back of his shirt. Just plain black, nothing discernable.

Squinting closer, I find his hand is also visible. My blood goes cold. On the man's hand is our high school class ring. I can't make out the year, but the clunky item is unmistakable.

Steps outside my door have me hastily stuffing the items back into the giraffe and burying it into the bottom of my suitcase.

My bedroom door opens only moments later.

I was sure I locked that.

"Breakfast?" Darius's kind voice is a distraction from my train of thought.

Meeting his eyes I watch as an indecipherable emotion flashes across his face, before his typical easygoing smile is back in place.

"Sure." I shrug my agreement and follow him. "I have a question," I state as we walk to the kitchen.

"Okay." Darius doesn't turn back.

I find myself tracing the line of his shoulders, the way his lean muscles push against the fabric. While he is the smallest of the brothers, he still towers over my frame. His hair is the darkest and longest of all the O'Briens and it falls in soft waves stopping just above his shoulders. I'm so mesmerized by the way it moves as he walks that I almost forget my question.

"Why did you drop out?" I finally get it out as we step into the kitchen. I am thankful neither of the other brothers are to be found.

Darius gestures for me to sit at the kitchen bar. I drag the stool out slowly and it's not until he is setting a plate in front of me that he answers, "Money."

The word isn't what I expected.

Darius settles on the other side of the counter leaning back and gesturing for me to eat.

I find myself studying my food. Eggs, salsa, bacon, and a pecan waffle. My favorites. Weird, but I shrug it off as a coincidence.

"When our grandmother passed, we no longer had her monthly income to help with bills," Darius continues.

I swallow a few bites before looking back up. Darius is staring at me intently. He seems both pleased and exasperated.

"I think you know, but we own the old marina. The money is okay, but Grayson needed the extra help. Axel and Tripp weren't available. I was."

"But..." I start, I'm suddenly annoyed for Darius. He is my age, but already he's forced to take care of himself, of his family.

I suddenly feel incredibly small. My parents may be sending money, but would it be enough? Should I be contributing in some way?

I am so self-absorbed. They just lost their brother and here I am in a full-blown pity party because I was forced to stay here. No, because I decided to live here instead of my grandmother's. They owed me nothing and it was my own anxieties making me look at these men in a bad light. What have any of the three actually done to me?

My stomach sours, and I carefully set my fork down.

"No, you're going to eat the rest of that." Grayson's voice cuts through the room causing me to jump in my seat.

"Gray," Darius acknowledges. "We agreed–"

"Talk to Axel," Grayson cuts him off, turning to me. "Eat your food and for fuck's sake don't try to sneak out in the middle of the night, and then fall asleep on the roof. It isn't safe. I have to work, but Darius is going to stay to keep an eye on you." Grayson and Darius exchange an unreadable look.

Feeling properly admonished, I pick up the fork and continue picking at my food.

Grayson takes another step until he is in my space. His tall frame towers over me, and he unexpectedly reaches down and softly tucks a curl that has escaped behind my ear as I chew. I find myself leaning into his firm hand. The feeling so incredibly familiar, and something inside me ignites.

The fork dropping to my plate has us both breaking from the moment.

He steps back and adjusts his shirt over his jeans. The jeans are sculpted to his thighs and I have to turn away from the intoxicating image.

"Be good for Darius. Please," Grayson grumbles before exiting the room.

I don't acknowledge him, he's treating me like a child and I don't like it, but I am beginning to suspect that is just who Grayson is. Controlling, overbearing, stern.

Some of me hates it, but the other part?

Guilt slithers up my spine as I try to refocus my attention on the breakfast ignoring how, once again, I reacted to another O'Brien brother. I am a horrible person, and nothing is making sense. How dare I *lust* after these brothers. How dare I feel this way. I let my hair fall back around my face as I finish my meal, using it as a shield between myself and the remaining O'Brien that watches me with his eagle eyes.

June 21st

Last night my plan was straightforward, but now I have a better idea in mind.

I finally finish my breakfast and look up to see Darius's sharp attention still focused on me. It makes me uncomfortable, but clearly, I will not be sneaking anywhere.

"Veronica said Auggie got a graduation present for me and I couldn't find it in our house. The last place I can think to look is the car...will you take me to the impound lot, please?" I ask hopefully. Darius doesn't owe me anything, he could just say no.

A soft regretful look graces Darius's features and he finally moves from where he has been leaning this entire time. "Come on, let's go."

The impound lot is depressing, dark, and dreary. A stark comparison to the weather that is currently bright and sweltering. The barbed wire fence is menacing and higher than I have any possible ability to scale and climb.

The ride over was a silent affair, minus the sound of his truck rumbling along to our destination. Darius hasn't even looked in my direction, he simply drives us here. His only discernible discomfort in this impromptu trip is his tight, white-knuckled grip on the steering wheel.

I walk up to the guard station that is separating me from, I'm not even exactly sure what. What do I expect?

A beefy older man steps out as I approach, a clipboard in hand. He wheezes with every step he takes.

"Hi, I am here to pick up my brother's items."

"His name?" the guard harrumphs out.

"Augustus Masch." I turn to see Darius approaching, he is watching the entire interaction with narrowed eyes. He seems on *edge*. "And Tripp O'Brien. I want to take a look at the car, too."

The guard flips through the pages of the clipboard, he is clearly annoyed at my arrival. I try to look through the gate to see if I can see my brother's familiar car, but there are too many vehicles to be able to pinpoint it.

"Hang tight. What's your name?" the guard eventually huffs out.

I go to answer, but Darius interjects, "Darius O'Brien."

The guard casts us both an irritable look before stepping back into his station.

I go to question Darius, but before I can, he places his hands on my shoulders and steps up behind me.

"Trust me, okay?" he leans down and whispers the words directly into my ear. His hair tickles my neck and I try to escape his grip. He won't let me. "Just wait for him."

I don't want to listen to anything Darius says, but I am in way over my head. I am teetering on the cusp of a breakdown; I can feel it. I want my graduation present, but I also want something that will explain what my brother is doing with the photo. Maybe in the vehicle there will be a charger for the flip phone? If not, I have a plan for that too.

The guard's return jerks me out of my thoughts and Darius drops his grip from my shoulders. The guard is holding a small box in his arms.

"The items. Car is gone."

Darius takes the box from the man.

"What do you mean, gone?" That makes zero sense. If it's not here, where would it be?

The guard's face scrunches up in frustration. "Look, be happy we got the items out. You have questions about the car? Call the sheriff."

At that the man is stomping off, panting as he goes.

"It was probably just the insurance picking the car up." I watch Darius's face as he speaks the words.

Why did Veronica say the exact same thing?

I don't know how I know it, but he is hiding something from me. They both are. I take the box from him and start walking back to his car.

Once inside, I open it.

I don't hear when Darius joins me, or when he turns the car on, or even really notice when the AC blasts directly into my eyes.

I'm too busy staring down at the envelopes in the box, they are placed on top of various other items I recognize as a mix of Tripp and Auggie's. There are three envelopes. My vision blurs as, once more, tears make their way into my eyes. I wipe them away furiously.

Darius places a comforting hand on my knee. I can feel every callous as his thumb begins to stroke up and down, and I allow myself to fall into the comfort if only for one moment.

I realize that maybe while I can't fully trust Darius, I can at least talk to him. He's been kind, more so than Grayson or Axel. I chew my lip in anxiety wondering if I should tell him about Tripp and me, but before I make a decision, Darius removes his hand from my knee and grabs the envelopes out of the box.

He hands me two and takes the third for himself.

"I know," he says.

My heart beats rapidly in my chest. What exactly does he know?

"About you and Tripp," he answers my unspoken question. Darius's sharp eyes meet mine. His face is morphed in shadows and I can't discern exactly what he is feeling. "I saw you two, up on the roof." It feels like there's more to it, but I don't press him.

His words lift a weight off of me that I didn't even notice I was carrying. "You knew?" The words come out broken.

Before I understand what is happening, Darius is pulling me across the cab of his truck directly into his arms and his embrace. The box and envelopes drop to his floorboard.

He is the smallest of the brothers, the most lean, but enveloped into him like this, I can feel his strength. His sturdy grip holds me to him tightly, but even still, he is careful, soft, comforting. Darius is an enigma. He is a sweet man, but I can feel the harshness of his body.

And he lost his brother, just as I lost mine.

"Why do you all seem so okay?" I sob the words out into his chest as he pats my hair.

"We're not." I feel as he presses a soft kiss to my forehead before leaning back a bit to catch my eyes. For once I can see the endless sadness in him. "None of us are, but we aren't shy or unaccustomed to grief. Once you see something happen enough, you grow numb to it. Whether you want to or not. And even when I do feel the crippling weight of loss? I remember that this isn't what he wanted. Tripp wanted me to live, to be happy." Darius reaches up, wiping my eyes and pushing back my curls behind my ears. "He wanted you to be happy, too."

Darius leans over me and grabs the envelopes off the floorboard. He hands me the one from Tripp first.

"Open it, if you're ready."

I'm not, but I still carefully unseal it, pulling out the piece of paper.

Hi Sunflower,

It's official; you are my graduated girl. I love you! I hope you know that the next step of life is going to be even more fun. And remember no matter what, do what makes you happy.

—Your Starboy

The last words from a dead man. I choke back my grief.

Short and to the point; very Tripp-like.

Do what makes you happy.

It's hard to even know what that is anymore, except that isn't true.

I'm not sure if it's happiness, but his brothers are making me feel *something*. It is more than anything else since Tripp and Auggie died. The brothers cause my heart to speed up, my nerves to turn to static, and all rational thought to leave me.

I didn't want to acknowledge it, but I knew what it was pointing to. What my reactions meant. It reminded me of when I first hung out with Tripp.

Crushes.

I was developing small, disgusting, unwanted crushes on the brothers. All three of them.

Stomping that thought down and the shame that came with it, I carefully fold the letter back up and go to reach for the other, but Darius holds onto it. "Maybe one at a time?"

I nod my head lethargically and he releases the envelope into my hand.

Moving slowly back to my side of the truck, I untangle myself from Darius, welcoming the distance, I need it to clear my mind. I drop both envelopes carefully back into the box.

Darius spares me one last look before driving away.

"My brother didn't have car insurance." No longer distracted by my own guilt, I state the words that have been bouncing around my brain. They said the car was taken by the insurance company, both Veronica and Darius. But they should both know my brother didn't have car insurance, at least not any for his own vehicle. No one should have taken his car. It doesn't make any sense.

Darius stiffens and if I weren't watching for his reaction, I might not have noticed the pure unfiltered terror that sweeps across his features before he schools his face and offers up a shrug.

We're at a stop light now. At an intersection I recognize. We're less than a mile from the accident site, even closer if I cut through the woods. I promised myself I wouldn't go, but there are so many things that keep tugging at me. Making me feel this isn't right.

How did Auggie, the notorious grandpa driver, lose control of the car? It was raining but that just means he would have been extra careful.

I was so focused on my own guilt in their accident, I never stopped to think how unusual it was in the first place.

Auggie would never have hydroplaned off the road and down the embankment. The car shouldn't be missing, there was no insurance claim to file, no reason for it to be taken. And the flip phone... the photo... the girl in it.

The more I discover, the less anything makes sense. My mind is working overtime trying to understand all the pieces, how any of it fits together.

If it even does.

But there is one place I haven't gone. Somewhere that might just have the answers I need.

My hands are shaking in anxiety, my breath ricocheting around my lungs, my heart pounding a beat in my ears. The light turns green and before I can think it through, I jump out of the truck and sprint away into the woods. My feet slapping beats against the ground as I push myself as fast as I can towards the last place I thought I would ever go.

All I hear in the background is Darius cursing and cars honking behind him.

June 21st

The run through the woods takes more out of me than I care to admit, but when I make it to the crash site, I can immediately tell something isn't right.

Exiting the woods, I cross the street to the edge of the embankment where my brother's car went off. It's on the corner of a sharp bend. Accidents have happened here before, and looking down, I can see the evidence of the vehicle's landing below: broken limbs, tire marks, at the bottom I can even make out parts of the car that were left behind. But that's not what is off.

There aren't any skid marks. No indication that he even tried to brake.

What's more, there's shattered red reflective glass all around. Sure it could have come from another car, but as I reach down I find red tape on one of the pieces.

Auggie had broken one of his lights and instead of getting it fixed, we had put this tape on it.

I drop the piece to the ground in shock.

Before I can investigate any further the squeal of tires causes me to look up. I expect to see Darius's truck.

Not Maxwell Thorne's black BMW.

I am frozen in shock as the car skids up. It stops when he is right beside me, blocking me off in the curve of the road, trapping me on the edge with a very long drop behind me. After a few beats he rolls the window down. "Whatcha doing all the way out here Sunday School?"

His tone is mocking, hateful. I can't make out anyone else in the car with him and the hairs on the back of my neck prick up. I don't want to be near this man. Especially not alone.

He reaches through the window and snags me by the front of my shirt before I can make my escape, but there really isn't anywhere to go. I'm stuck between his car and a two-hundred-foot drop. I stumble forward and use my hands to catch me from tumbling through his window. I hadn't noticed it before, but now that I'm looking for it, I see he's wearing a class ring.

Just like the man in the picture.

Was it him?

"I don't know." The words come out less sure than I intended, and I watch as a sinister smile spreads across Maxwell's face.

"Well, why don't I give you a *ride*?"

My anxiety thickens and my mouth goes dry. This man is dangerous.

"Let her go," Grayson's rough voice cuts through my fear. Even though I can't see him from my vantage point, I immediately find my anxiety dissipating as if everything is going to be okay.

Maxwell is sneering at me, our faces are still only a few inches apart. I can feel his hot breath and smell the alcohol on him. "Oh, look here, you never could take care of yourself, could you?" Maxwell pushes me back.

I'm so close to where Auggie's car went off the road that for a sick moment when I lose my balance, terror shoots down my spine, but before I can topple backward into the ravine, Grayson suddenly appears around the car and is reaching out and pulling me towards him. Into the safety of his arms.

Maxwell doesn't say anything else, instead he peels away, missing us both by inches.

"You, okay?" Grayson's gruff voice is thick with an indecipherable emotion. He straightens me up and does a once over of my body as if checking for injury. His clothes are covered in grease, his hair is in disarray. He clenches his tattooed hands into fists when his examination makes it to my shirt.

I look down at the fabric and see it has torn a bit from Maxwell's handling.

I don't want to meet Grayson's eyes. Today has been an emotional day without the added guilt of his judgment. "What aren't you all telling me?" I stare at the red reflective plastic with tape on it lying on the ground as I ask the question that has been eating at me since the memorial. "How are you here?" How do they know when I need them? I don't have the courage to voice the last part. It means admitting that I do need them.

I finally look up at Grayson's depthless light eyes. The hazel is more noticeable in the sun's setting rays. He is exhausted. It is written in code into his very being, as if every piece of him is held together with glue. I realize I never humanized Grayson before, he was always just *the older brother*. But in this moment as the sun slowly sinks on the horizon, as I stand just a few inches apart from the man, I come to a stark realization. Grayson is tired and *lonely*.

I don't notice I am moving until my hand reaches up to cup his cheek, he leans into it and the scratchiness of his beard tickles a bit. He closes his eyes and lets out a shuddering sigh.

"I don't know how to answer you without it not making any sense. I just need you to trust us. If you see the Thorne brothers—Maxwell and Rayden—their friend Mark, or the sheriff's son, William, please just run.

Run as far away from them as you can and when you think you've run far enough? Keep going. They aren't good men."

I understand Maxwell Thorne, but why would I need to keep away from his older brother, Rayden? He's harmless. I start to drop my hand, but Grayson reaches up, placing his much larger one, on top of mine. Pressing my palm further along his jaw. My hand is sandwiched between his hardened face and rough fingers. Grayson bends down, watching me the entire time. I am unsure of what his move is, and I don't get a chance to find out as the notorious sound of Darius's truck approaches us.

Grayson doesn't jump back, but I watch as something shifts across his face. He lets go of my hand and it drops weakly between us. He places a chaste kiss on my forehead. "One day, this will all make sense, but please, until then, be safe? Don't run off without us."

June 21st

This has been another long fucking day.

Darius is fuming. No longer is he the easy-going brother. I have officially gotten under his skin. "Why do you insist on making irrational decisions?"

The truck bounces as he jerks us down the road, we aren't far from their house. I don't answer him, I am deep in thought over everything that has happened.

The letters, the car, the accident, the photo, Maxwell, the class ring... *Grayson.*

After Darius's arrival they exchanged a look before Grayson walked to his car on the side of the road and left as if nothing had even happened.

"And now you can't even bother to respond? Do you have some kind of death wish?" He slams on the brakes, and it finally rockets me out of my swirling brain.

I meet his eyes and see that he is just worried, but I can't help but be annoyed. They are lying to me. They are hiding something from me. I know it just as I know that the picture has something to do with Auggie and Tripp's death. It is an innate feeling that I can't discern or describe.

My face must show my annoyance, because Darius calms himself, he rubs his temples and closes his eyes. "We just want to keep you safe. I wish you could understand that we aren't the enemy."

But that's the thing, I have very little reason to trust them other than our shared grief. They have been good to me these last two days, but is that enough to really know them or their intentions. But for now? I guess that will have to be enough. "Truce?" I offer up my hand for him to shake.

I can tell he doesn't believe me, but sometimes we force ourselves to believe lies in order to feel better. In order to feel more secure.

He tenderly takes my hand and gives it a soft squeeze before letting it go. I ignore the way my skin tingles everywhere that he touched and wipe it against my shirt.

Darius follows the movement, his eyes darkening just like Grayson's had at the ripped fabric. "If nothing else, can we agree Maxwell is bad news?"

"Yes." That is something I am willing for us to come to an understanding on. Maxwell makes me feel gross, just the thought of him is reminiscent of a snake slithering across my skin.

I offer Darius one more reassuring smile, before grabbing the box from the impound lot, and hopping out of the truck. As I go to close the door behind me, I notice that Darius's envelope from his brother still sits on the dashboard.

Unopened.

I make it up to my room without any further encounters with the O'Brien brothers. Leaning on the back of the wooden bedroom door, I finally relax. Releasing the tension in my shoulders I hadn't noticed was there. The physical separation from the brothers is a necessity. While I don't believe they wish to harm me, I know something isn't right.

The box weighs heavily in my hands. I walk the few feet to the bed, setting it down and settling carefully next to it. I take the two envelopes first, placing them carefully on my nightstand. I don't have the mental capacity to open the one from Auggie. Yet.

Rifling through the box, I find that it's mostly just clothes. I'm almost surprised to see no blood on the items–they must have been kept in the trunk of the car. Neither of their phones are in the box though. Another oddity. Auggie's phone hadn't been returned to us. The next item I pull out, I recognize as Tripp's sweater. I place the soft material against my face and breathe it in. A mixture of his deodorant and natural woodsy smell invades my senses.

I don't know how long I am cradling the sweater to my face, but eventually my phone's vibrations jolt me out of my haze.

It's Carrie. Should I tell her about Maxwell? About my suspicions? Would she even believe me?

"Sunday!! Hey, I miss you. You been doing okay?" Her words are cheerful enough, but I can hear an underlying tone of exhaustion.

I snort softly into the phone. It's only been three days, but I wonder if she even remembers the night of the party. I wish I could forget it. "Hey Carrie, doing my best. What's up?" I don't want to weigh her down with the pressure of my pain and loneliness. She is trying to be nice, she is trying to be a good friend. It's not her fault that her boyfriend is a terrifying piece of shit that decided to put me in his cross fire.

I resolve to mention it to her, try to be a good friend and warn her about him, but I don't get a chance. She keeps chugging right along, "River day coming up!! You have to come. We're going to post up in the spot behind William's house." She lowers her voice a bit and it no longer holds its previous peppy tone. "You know you can talk to me, right? I don't fully understand, but I do care about you. And I always cared about your brother even after we split."

My heart warms a bit. Once more, Carrie is offering a branch to me. She and I have hung out since our freshman year when she started dating my brother. They were together until the middle of our junior year. They seemed to have a great relationship, but they broke up out of the blue. They did end up staying friends, but I know it hurt her when he ended up dating Veronica as soon as he went off to college, but she never let it show. Carrie is also partially the reason why Tripp and I ended up together. Tripp was tired of being a third wheel so they started to invite me along too.

I change my mind, maybe it's best I don't tell her about Maxwell, not on the phone at least. I want to be a friend to her, but I want to wait until we're in person together. Where I can gauge her reaction.

Does she know who Maxwell is? Or is she ignorantly unaware?

The river day. I shouldn't go to this event, but I know I am going to. I have to get answers, and William's house is right next to where they'll be partying on the river. Maybe I can search his house and find the evidence I need. "Yeah, that sounds fun. When is it?"

Carrie's light tone returns. "July 4th..." she hesitates, I can tell there's more.

"What is it?"

"Are you really living with *them?* With the O'Briens?"

I don't like her tone, but I can't blame her. Tripp was the golden child, the *good* brother. The rest are known for being a drop-out, a felon, and well, I wasn't exactly sure what Grayson was known for, but it wasn't good. "I am," I confirm. "But it's okay, they mostly leave me alone. My parents are away for work." I'm not sure why I am defending them, but it feels right to do so. "I'll be there though for the river day, thank you for inviting me."

Again, she pauses but this time she decides not to press the matter. "Sounds good, Sunday, but seriously, if you ever need me, I am just one call away."

I appreciate the sentiment, but something about this entire conversation has been incredibly off-putting and draining.

I am beginning to suspect that maybe our friendship has run its course.

June 22nd

*W**ater ripples all around me, pressing me further and further into its depths. I try to breathe, but instead of air or even water, my airway is greeted with sediment. I try to cough the material up, but it fills up my mouth and nose.*

I am facedown in the water, being shoved into the ground below. Large hands compress on my back and I feel as my lungs protest. I attempt to thrash about, but the hands don't budge, instead they push heavier onto me. I feel the full weight of the person above as I am drowned in the shallow water.

I know the moment I am dead.

My body no longer cooperates, and the hands let me go. I hear the splashing of my murderer's retreat as I lie there unable to do anything.

"Oh Sunflower, not again," the voice caresses my ear, swirling in my subconscious.

Someone's grip pulls me out of my shallow grave, and while I still can't move or function, I can now see my surroundings.

I am on the bend of a river, but more importantly, I am staring directly into my brother's eyes. I cannot process how it makes me feel, especially not in this state.

"We have to stop meeting here." He smiles softly, he wipes my face off, but I feel nothing.

It's at that point, I realize that it's not his hold keeping me up. "Sunflower, please, you have to let this go. Let us go. It's going to be okay. They're going to take care of you. You just need to be happy. Before it's too late." Tripp's voice is a familiar gentle breeze into my ear.

Suddenly I feel everything. The pain of my death, the agony of loss, the desperation to return to Auggie and Tripp.

My vision fades and I wake up to the sound of screaming. It takes five seconds to realize that the noise is coming from me. Another ten seconds to notice I am wrapped in an embrace.

"Hush, it's going to be okay." Axel's gruff words are muffled by my hair.

He is cradling and rocking me in his large muscular arms and before I know it, he has us rolled so I am on top of him. I am forced to place my hands on his shoulders to catch myself from falling.

"What... what's going on?" I am barely awake, this feels surreal as if it's part of the dream I just had. Or was it a nightmare? The memory of it is fading faster than they normally do, but it felt so familiar, as if I had been in that dream more times than I knew.

Establishing myself in reality, I jump to escape from Axel's body, but he catches me by the waist before I can move away.

"Stop," he growls the word. "You stubborn girl, just stay with me. Just let me be here for you. You're not as goddamn alone as you want to think you are."

The unmistakable length of his cock pushes against me and in my sleep riddled state, I find myself rolling subconsciously against it.

He hisses as he thrusts upward. His rough fingers find the skin under my shirt, drifting slowly until gripping me tightly on my waist, his thumbs rubbing my back. "Now is not the time for that. Be a good Little Lamb, let me take care of you. And at the end of it? You don't have to feel guilty. You can blame the monster. You can say I made you feel the way you do."

I don't understand what he's saying or what he means. I am raw. His touch is scorching, lighting me on fire. My emotions are haywire and nothing is making any sense to me. I just want to go back to sleep and forget that this world exists. Forget that I am here living it, alone. Because he's wrong, there isn't anyone that loves me. I am officially in a pity-party of one, but I don't care.

I don't even question why he's in my room. The room I know for a fact I locked the door to this time. Axel is wrong about a lot of things, but there's one that he's right about.

He is the monster under my bed. And I so desperately want someone to blame. Want someone to fight.

My want to escape twists into a desire to fight instead. Fury ripples along my skin, heating a path as it goes.

Now I am pounding my fists against his chest, yelling at him, cursing at him. He takes it all in stride, he doesn't even flinch.

"What a good Little Lamb, I am everyone's scapegoat, everyone's supposed monster and for that I am incredibly angry and enraged. But when it comes to you? I would be that and more. You just have to let me in."

He's flipping us and pulling down my shorts before I even know what's happening.

"Pretend whatever you want, blame whoever you want. But just feel. Let yourself feel good. And then tomorrow when you wake up and you're enveloped in guilt, you can hate me again, but I still won't regret it."

That's the only warning I get before he moves down the bed, before his face is between the apex of my thighs, before he consumes me.

My breath stutters, it takes longer than I care to admit to even *want* to push him away.

He licks up and down and brings his large strong hands up to my thighs separating them further and resting them over his shoulders. With his hands free, he uses one to push past my folds into me, and the other he grips onto my hip to hold me in place. My desire pulses, a spring coiling, building up, I am nearing an edge that I know I shouldn't fall over.

It's time to fight him. Time to pretend I am not loving every moment of this. That I am not a horrible, terrible person. Less than a month ago, I was dating his twin. His now *dead* twin. But his touch is igniting me in a way that I have never felt before. Everything about Axel exudes passion, madness. An explosion seconds from going off. He is making me feel good, too *good*.

"Get out of that beautiful mind of yours. Stop thinking." He bites down on my clit and it has the wanted effect. I feel myself trembling from his treatment as heat curls deep in my belly. "One day soon, it won't just be my fingers stretching this pretty little cunt of yours," Axel promises as he crooks them into me, pushing at a point just inside that causes me to let out a desperate gasp of air.

"Axel." The word was supposed to come out as a warning, but it is husky and saturated with want and need.

I push my guilt to the very back of my mind as I give in to the most dangerous of the O'Brien brothers.

I reach down and I hold onto his long soft hair pushing his mouth further onto my clit.

He adds another finger as he continues to push them in and out, he seems to know exactly where he needs to press and every spot that makes shockwaves shoot across my nerves. I am edging the precipice.

"Fuck," he says the word against my clit. The vibrations, his fingers, the pressure, his firm grip on my hip bone. They push me over the edge.

I come with a cry. Lifting up off of the bed and trembling around his fingers, they don't let up. Instead he quickens his speed for the next several moments as wave after wave crashes through me.

He doesn't stop until I am panting on the bed. A mess.

I watch as he pulls his fingers out of me and his face away.

I am not the only mess.

Before he gets too far, he leans back down, and I feel as he begins to suck on the inside of my thigh with bruising pressure.

It feels good. Too good. I let out a soft moan of appreciation.

He pulls back causing a popping noise to come from his mouth detaching from my thigh. Axel stands up, a fierce smile on his harsh features. "Mine." He puts his wet fingers into his mouth and sucks my essence off of them. "Tasty Little Lamb, aren't you?"

The scene is intoxicating and a soft gasp leaves me at the sight.

His face darkens. "Blame me for that, but just know, I am nowhere near done with you. Grayson and Darius? They want to treat you with kid gloves." He leans over the bed, his lips inches from mine, his bright eyes searing into my soul. "But not me, I am here to push your limits. To make you realize, everything that you need is right in front of your face."

He's made me a raw emotional mess, but I find that I like it. That underneath the guilt something else entirely is pulsating. I feel alive, content, satisfied. Axel makes me feel like I am the center of his universe.

I can smell myself on him and I want to taste it. I arch my back to do just that.

The thought and action startle me.

As if Axel is a mind reader, he is pushing forward, his lips capturing mine. The combined taste of us is heady. He reaches forward, catching my curls and holding me in place. He is all sharpness, control, power. He is dominating me.

It's nowhere near how Tripp treated me.

Tripp.

The guilt returns twofold, and I push against his chest. He lets me.

A feral grin spreads across his face. "See you around, little girl."

He leaves the room before I can even begin to unravel what has happened. What we just did. How he made me feel. *Alive. Wanted.*

Shame churns in my gut, up my throat, making it difficult to breathe. Air leaves my lips in short pants as I come to a startling realization.

I want more of whatever he has to offer.

June 22nd

It's not long before I fall back to sleep. I don't dream of anything else, and when I wake up in the morning, I am alone.

I have accepted that I am a terrible person. I betrayed Tripp. With his own brother. His *twin* brother. The thought is sobering as I slowly throw on clean clothes.

My eyes flicker to the box of items they left behind—I have returned the two letters to it now—and then to where I put the giraffe.

Before the river day, I am going to find a charger for the phone, but until then? Well I am not exactly sure what my plan is.

Dressed, I exit my room. I shove my hands into my short's pockets, my eyes flicker about, my lungs constrict making it difficult to breathe. I am on edge, I don't know what I would do if I run into Axel, but conveniently, I never seem to see him during the daytime.

He would *make a good vampire; except he's always entering spaces unwelcomed.*

The thought causes an uninhibited laugh to leave my lips, and it shocks me.

I can't remember the last time I laughed.

I smell the bacon before I enter the kitchen. Darius is eating at the counter, his laptop in front of him.

He looks up, gifting me a strained smile. "Sleep okay?"

The question has my face flushing, did he hear me? Know that I was *with* Axel? The embarrassment and shame roll in equal waves along my nerves. I decide I am in fact, not hungry, but before I can make my escape he continues.

"You were screaming," he offers up softly.

Oh. "Nightmare." I shrug a shoulder and eye the plate of food on the counter.

"For you," he confirms.

My heart swells. Darius is continuously feeding me, making sure I am okay, he even got me a birthday cupcake. He is the least dangerous of the brothers and I really ought to be nicer to him.

Even if he is hiding something from me.

"Thanks." I grab the plate and settle down next to him. I glance over at the laptop he is concentrating on. I can't hide the shock when I see what he's doing.

"Online classes," Darius confirms, his attention focused on the screen.

"For high school?" I put a bite of food into my mouth, chewing carefully.

"Local college. I already have my GED. I didn't actually drop out, I got it and then left school." He appears to be taking a test, but he's answering the questions too quickly to even read. Or maybe he is just that smart.

"Oh." Once more I listened to rumors and let other people's opinions cloud my judgment. "I shouldn't have taken a year off." I'd been having the thought since my parents left. My best friend, Julia, was off on vacation. She was supposed to be my roommate in college, the same college Tripp and Auggie went to.

I needed to reach out to her. I felt bad, I hadn't really talked to her since everything happened, but even before that, our friendship had been strained. Cracks breaching through as they often do when you keep secrets from each other. Hers, the party she went to over winter break and mine... Tripp.

I was almost grateful she skipped the graduation ceremony to go on a trip with her parents and seemed to have shoddy cell service. It was an excuse to not contact her. To not break the news that I wouldn't be joining her anymore.

Darius clicks *submit* on the test, and I am able to see he receives a perfect score before he shuts his laptop and gifts me with his attention. "No, you need time to process everything. It's good to take a break."

I don't point out how hypocritical the statement is. "Sure." I finish up eating and he takes both our plates.

When he is done loading them into the dishwasher he turns to me. "What about we have a movie marathon?"

My eyebrows shoot up. While the brothers are clearly invading my life, it's odd for him to offer to *hang out* with me. It throws me off. "Sure." This time the word comes out unsteadily.

Darius returns to my side and offers me a hand. I timidly take it.

The second our fingers touch, déjà vu skitters down my spine. A foggy memory that doesn't take on any substance and dissipates as soon as it appears.

"Why do I feel like I have known you longer? That this isn't the first time we've done this?" The questions come out before I can think how crazy they might sound.

Darius drops my hand as if it burns. His eyebrows draw together and his mouth opens on an O. He looks freaked out, concerned, worried. He forces out a laugh but it doesn't convince either of us.

I push past the weirdness and add it to the never-ending list of things that just aren't right.

Nothing has really been right since Tripp and Auggie's death.

Darius leads the way to the living room. I relax into the comfortable couch leaving him space as he sets up the marathon.

"Any requests?" he asks.

"Nothing scary." I look down at my legs and realize that my movements have pulled my shorts up.

Axel left his mark.

The bruise on my thigh is dark and discolored. A testament to my sins. A startled noise leaves me at the sight of it.

Darius whips his head from the TV to me. His focus follows my own and zeroes in on the bruise. His mouth forms a tight line, and I watch as his fists clench. I can't decipher his reaction, but I feel bare.

I find a blanket and pull it up, wrapping myself in its comfort. Covering my mistakes.

Darius's eyes meet mine. "Axel," he spits the word, before turning back to the TV.

I don't acknowledge it.

He puts on a scary movie, but I don't argue. I don't know if he did it maliciously or because he was distracted.

My face is heated in embarrassment, and I can use the blanket to hide from the worst parts.

If only a blanket worked on the scary parts of life.

He sits next to me at the other end of the couch and puts my feet in his lap. We sit like that in uncomfortable silence for the entire movie. When it's finally over, I just want to leave. To crawl into the bath and relax, unwind, steady myself.

Darius sighs heavily, the noise has me jumping. The blanket falls and he is hyper focused on the bruise once more. I think he can tell my discomfort because he puts the blanket back in place before encapsulating my feet in his hands, rubbing them one at a time.

His long fingers keep massaging my feet. Human touch–it feels comforting. I allow myself to relax into him.

"We all agreed, you know? Even Tripp. That we wouldn't try to date you. We promised Auggie we wouldn't."

The statement is nowhere near what I expected him to say, his hands travel up my feet to my legs, stroking and massaging as he goes.

He quirks his lips.

"Imagine my surprise when I saw you up on your roof, kissing him. When I heard you sneak into his room. It's right next to mine." His tone is harsh.

"I...I didn't know. I thought no one knew. I thought we were waiting to tell my brother after I graduated—on my birthday—it made sense."

His hands have made their way under the blanket and up to my knees, I try to ignore the sensations his calloused fingers bring forth. No longer do I find it relaxing, now an entirely different feeling takes hold.

It tingles and ignites as he strokes the outside of my thighs.

Suddenly, he stops.

"Axel promised." I don't have time to examine what that means. Darius moves swiftly. He's now hovering over me, encapsulating my entire body, his hair falling in a halo. His face inches from mine. We breathe the same breath for a few moments and I stay frozen. Unknown emotions are suffocating me. With Darius it's different. I feel differently. He has in a short time become reliable, safe, comfortable. He is a place to return.

I care about him.

The thought is jarring. I don't understand how I have grown to care about him so quickly.

"Come back to me." He leans down. Our foreheads touch, his hair tickles my nose, his haunted eyes watching me cautiously. And then softly, ever so carefully, he presses his lips onto mine; they are soft, firm, unyielding. He gently pushes into my mouth his tongue flicking out. I didn't realize until this moment that it's pierced. The metal ball is cold against my tongue and the dichotomy in temperature causes a shiver to roll through me. Darius presses further into my body, I can feel his cock against me, and I find myself wanting to push up into him to get the friction I need.

He lets up, pulling back. Detangling our mouths, he stops only centimeters away. "You know that I am always here for you if you need me, right?"

My eyes meet his, this moment feels so incredibly tender, and I cannot help the way his words pierce me. How they add to the flush that spreads across my cheeks, how I want nothing more than to go further with this man. Darius is the calm before a storm, the eye of a hurricane, the silence before a predator strikes. He is comfort, but there's an edge to it, as if something is coming, but I just don't know what it is yet.

I stare into his eyes desperately trying to portray to him exactly how he is making me feel, but then the guilt hits me, a violent slap to the face.

His face shutters. "'These violent delights have violent ends. And in their triumph die, like fire and powder, which as they kiss consume. The sweetest honey,'" he murmurs the quote against my lips. "I'm sorry, I just needed to remind myself that you're real. That you're here."

My heart is beating rapidly in my chest, but I don't have time to work through what has just happened, as a throat clearing grabs my attention. I can see another O'Brien brother over Darius's shoulder.

Grayson is clearly pissed. He's standing at the edge of the living room. His brow is scrunched, his lips are flat, he's rubbing his forehead, he's tapping his foot.

"Darius," he remarks before he turns and walks to the kitchen.

I refocus on the youngest brother. His eyes are on mine. Adoration in their depths. It scares me. I look away, waiting for him to get up, to move off of me.

He doesn't.

"Go," I say. I need him to leave so I can break down. Alone and in peace. Let the guilt win. Blame my grief for kissing not one, but two of the remaining O'Brien brothers.

He nuzzles into my neck. "I'm not going to push you, I am going to be your friend. But I also care about you, more than you realize. We all do. This isn't something to feel bad about. Tripp knew." He kisses my hair, dropping that bomb before finally getting up off me and leaving me more confused than before.

Tripp knew? Knew what exactly? Nothing is making any sense. *Again*.

I watch his retreat and when he is fully out of sight, I get up myself.

I go to walk to my room, but shouting redirects my attention towards the men. I can't hear anything decipherable, except as Darius stomps into the living room over his shoulder he yells back, "Take it up with Axel."

He grabs onto my hand and leads me up the stairs to his room. It is situated between where I currently reside and Tripp's. Opening the door, he pushes me softly inside. The room is dark, the curtains drawn, but I can see from the light of the stars on the ceiling.

The sight of them makes me smile, but the sound of his door clinking into place draws my attention.

"Let's just hibernate and watch movies. Nothing more. We can hang out and I will make us snacks. This is what makes me feel the best when I think too much and my mind won't stop racing. You've experienced a lot. And you are still dealing with the loss of both Tripp and Auggie." Darius offers up the explanation, switching on his TV and falling onto his bed. He pats the space next to him. "Friends?" He offers me his pinky.

I'm still so incredibly confused by everything that has happened these past few days, but there is one thing I really do need. A friend. I seal the promise with my pinky and carefully lay next to him in his bed. His silky sheets are comfy and his warm smell envelops me as I lean back carefully.

This time when he puts on a movie, it's a comedy.

And that's where I hide for the remainder of the day. Darius is right. In here with him and just the TV blaring, it's easy to forget how fucked up everything is.

I have formulated a plan to figure out what all is going on, but until then? I am going to accept any solace I can find.

Part II Bargaining and Depression

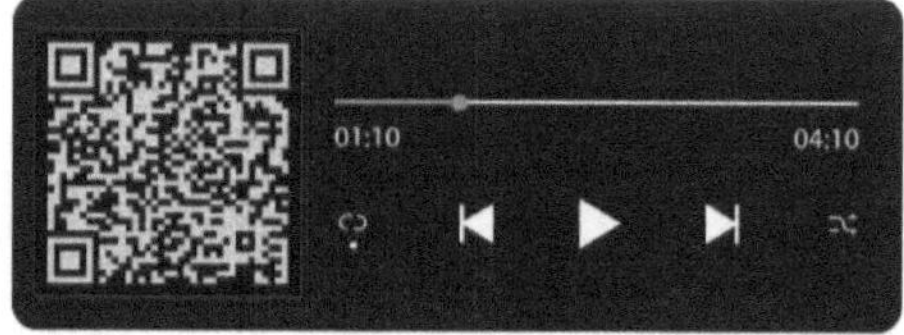

June 30th

Before I even know it, a routine forms. Every day I spend with Darius in companionable silence. He feeds me, we watch movies, TV shows, and just exist side by side. Every night I fall asleep in his bed. And every morning I wake up in my own.

The only discernible difference is sometimes, in the middle of the night after I am returned to my bed, I will rouse from a nightmare. And lying next to me? It's Axel on my bed, wrapped around me, holding me. When I wake in the morning though, he's always gone.

I begin to suspect that he doesn't sleep. Or maybe that's why I never see him during the daylight hours. He's catching up on all the time he spends watching me sleep. It should creep me out, but in some sick, twisted way, it makes me feel secure. Cared for. Less alone.

I don't see much of Grayson, but when I do, he offers nothing but tight-lipped smiles and shows his obvious discomfort.

Except right now.

I had completed the first part of my new routine and fallen asleep in Darius's bed, but for the first time I wake up while being carried back to my room. I expect Darius or even Axel, but it's Grayson that's holding me in his embrace. I'm tucked carefully against his chest and I can feel his strength, his rippling muscles, his large hands as he balances me to open my door. I can hear his heart's soothing beat as he shoulders it shut.

"I know you're awake," he says as he places me carefully into my bed. Axel isn't here. Yet.

I meet his eyes. Maybe it's the magic of the middle of the night, but his eyes are less guarded than usual. They almost appear soft.

He reaches down pulling the blanket over me, tucks my hair behind my ear, and places a gentle kiss to my forehead.

It melts my heart.

I reach forward before he can leave. Holding him by his pajama pants. "I'm sorry," I whisper the words out.

Whatever he expected me to say it wasn't that. "Why do *you* need to be sorry?"

"It's my fault that they're dead. I made them come." Even if it wasn't an accident, they were still there because of me. Darius has been doing a good job at distracting me, but in these moments, half awake and vulnerable, my pain is just as tangible as ever.

Grayson grumbles and bends down until he's staring directly into my eyes. "None of this is your fault. None of it. Everyday people make choices and unfortunately those choices come with consequences that affect more than themselves. Baby girl, if anything, I owe you an apology. I want to support you, to make sure you're okay, but I don't want to push you. I want to be someone you can rely on."

Tears form in my eyes, Grayson's voice is stern, but I begin to discern what I already knew. Grayson is both of his brothers' rock, but who is his?

I pat the bed next to me. "Will you keep me company?"

He hesitates.

"I don't want any more nightmares. *Please*?" The last word comes out as a whine.

He lets out a shuddering sigh before carefully sitting on the bed next to me. I grab onto him, pulling him to me.

My arms wrap around the much larger man, his form is almost too much for me to encapsulate, but I do my best.

"You don't have to be alone," I hum the words into his hair and he shakes against me.

I feel as tension releases from him and he relaxes into my embrace. He carefully returns the hug, wrapping me in his warmth. Grayson makes me feel like everything is going to be okay. That I am stronger than I really am. His loneliness somehow leaches away at my own.

"You are too kind, too pure. This world doesn't deserve you, baby girl." I can feel the heat of his words on my neck. Goosebumps prickle down my spine. I find myself suddenly incredibly hot. I want more from Grayson. I need what he has to offer. I need a release. Something to expel the excess tension that lives in my body. That seeps into my bones.

I jerk back abruptly, my wants at odds with my brain.

"I want to help. Darius said the marina needs more help—"

"No," Grayson cuts me off.

My temper flares, but I tamper it down. "I will go stir crazy in this house. I need more distractions. The movies and mindless TV are working for now, but I need more."

Grayson breathes out heavily and it moves some of his hair that has fallen into his hardened eyes. "Stubborn girl." He laughs humorlessly. "Sure why not, but Darius is coming with you."

My babysitter, of course, but I don't fight him on the matter. I'm excited, I've never had a real job, and while I don't know what to expect, I'm happy I'll be contributing. That I'll be doing something. Anything.

My eyes flicker to where the giraffe is hidden. Where the photo and flip phone are.

Soon I'll need to find out more, to investigate further, but in the meantime I'll be good.

Grayson doesn't get up, instead he draws me back into his arms, wrapping around me carefully.

I ignore when Axel creeps into the room. Grayson's only reaction is to pull me tighter to his body.

Axel grumbles but says nothing before wedging himself on the other side of me. That is where I fall asleep. Sandwiched between the brothers. Feeling happier than I have any right to be.

One month after Auggie and Tripp's death.

I'm sorry Tripp, I don't think this is the happiness you meant.

July 1st

I am hiding.

When I wake, both Axel and Grayson are gone, and now I don't know what to do. How to process either of the men. How to discern the difference between guilt and shame. Between right and wrong.

Except my growing feelings for these brothers? Well that is most assuredly wrong.

In order to distract myself, I decide it is time to get some answers.

I find the hiding place, grab the giraffe, and lock myself in the bathroom.

I put the stuffed animal up to my face and for a moment I just breathe in Auggie's scent. It calms my nerves and steadies me in the here and now.

Here I am in the bathroom, leaning against the counter, doing anything to not look at my reflection.

I am holding a picture and the phone. A very disgusting, ugly picture. An incredibly useless dead phone.

I turn the phone in my hands, press the button on the side. Nothing happens.

The charging port is circular in shape and I am unsure where I would find a charger that works for it.

But I have a different idea. Pulling out my own phone, I take the SIM card out and replace it with the one from the flip phone.

I restart my phone for measure and then give it a few minutes.

While it is working its magic, I take more time to examine the polaroid.

It looks like the picture is taken from a closet between two wooden panels. The girl I don't recognize is cast in shadows. She is lying on a bed, her limbs spread about, and her eyes are shut. There is just enough light to see she has a tattoo on the inside of her wrist that is closest to the person taking the picture. It's a very large yin and yang symbol.

Maybe she is a willing participant, but the way that she is lying and her expressionless face... I would guess she isn't.

From this angle, I can see the man's black shirt, bare ass, and his left hand on the bed. His head is completely out of the frame, and it's challenging to discern any distinguishable features.

It doesn't look like he has done anything.

Yet.

But his intentions are clear.

I wonder if my brother stopped it. Or if he let it play out a little further and has better proof. I shudder, I seriously hope he stepped in. That this poor girl doesn't have to live with an unbearable trauma.

A knife twists in my gut. How did my brother get this picture? How did he know he needed it?

Everything is screaming at me that the person in this picture is Maxwell. They have the same class ring for fuck's sake. But I have minimal proof and a grainy picture of the back of an ass, a back, and a single hand is not much to go on.

My phone lights up.

A knock on my bathroom door startles me.

"Sunday? You getting ready? We are meeting Grayson at the marina soon." Darius's voice holds an edge I am not used to.

"I'll be right out." I lean forward and flush the toilet.

He doesn't say anything else, and I listen for his retreat, but I don't hear it.

Fucking overbearing brothers.

I glance down at my phone, and I can see that there are several notifications. Ones that I desperately want to investigate but not with Darius feet away.

I still don't fully trust them. There is something in my gut pulsating with anxiety anytime I am near them.

I am *too* comfortable around them and as asinine as that sounds, it leaves me on edge.

I curse under my breath, I swap the SIM cards back, stuff the items into the giraffe and hide the stuffed animal in my tits.

Sorry, Auggie.

He would kill me if he were still alive for putting his precious stuffie there.

I wash my hands before stepping into my bedroom.

Darius looks up from the letter he has in his hands. It's the one from Tripp.

He has a distant, wistful smile on his face. And for a moment he looks much older than his age.

"Tripp always did have a way with words," he laughs jokingly.

I step forward and go to take the letter from him, but with his free hand, he catches me by the wrist.

His dark critical eyes trap mine as he sets the letter down and slowly pulls me to him until I am standing in between his thighs.

With him sitting, I don't have to look down; we are eye level. I enjoy the equal footing. It feels like less of a power imbalance.

I am not sure what I expect him to do, but it's definitely not pat me down.

His free hand taps both my front pockets first and then my back ones.

Annoyance shrouds his features. "But Tripp had one thing wrong–" Darius stops his obvious search of my person and instead catches me by the chin forcing me to stare into the depth of his eyes "–you're not a sunflower, you're a *wildflower*." He seals his words with a kiss. His hot breath is the only warning I get before his full lips are pressing against mine. One hand catches in my curls, the other holds me by the waist as he deepens it.

His tongue pokes at the seam of my lips and even though I am expecting it, the coldness of his piercing causes me to gasp. He takes it as an invitation.

He is pushing into me, feeding from me, intoxicating me.

I feel like I am both underwater and up in the clouds.

After a few more moments one of his hands moves to cup my breasts and clarity punctures my thoughts. I pull away struggling for air. Was that a farce to search me? Confusion and unease crawl across my skin.

"Stop," I manage to wheeze out.

He immediately drops his hands, halting his exploration.

I won't meet his eyes. I don't want him to see the emotions that are swirling in mine, the suspicion. "You pinkie promised."

"I know." Darius leans forward, kissing my nose before standing up directly into my space. He stares down at me.

I refuse to meet his eyes.

He pecks the top of my head. "We're still *friends*." He finally puts space between us and I am able to breathe again.

I don't watch him as he heads to the door, but I hear him pause before he closes it. "Get dressed, *Wildflower*."

Chapter 20
July 1st

It's summer in the south, and I should have expected that the marina might be crowded, but I am still thoroughly surprised when Darius and I arrive to a full parking lot, after a silently awkward ride over.

The marina isn't the main source of crowd though, it is actually the restaurant above, which is where we are headed now.

The restaurant itself looks like it is made out of old boats and anything you can find in a junkyard, but once inside, the smell is *amazing*. My mouth instantly salivates and I am innately aware I have not eaten yet today.

Darius, who apparently knows more about me than I know myself, takes me to the one empty spot in the restaurant.

A booth in the corner with a sign on it: "Reserved."

He pushes me gently down first, and I continue looking around as I sit.

It's weird to be out in the real world. It's weird that time didn't just stop because my brother died, because Tripp died. People are just here going about their day without a care in the world. All of the tables are full and the noise ricochets off the paneled walls.

A full room, and again, I feel alone.

I am grateful for the location of the booth, because once I am settled down and slide all the way in, I can't see anyone and hopefully that means they can't see me either.

"Hang tight, I'll get you some food," Darius promises. He offers me one last wary look before walking towards the kitchen.

It feels like less than a minute later that a newcomer is sliding into the booth across from me.

It's not someone I want to see.

"William." The word is laced in disgust and my face hardens.

"Sunday," William's voice comes out softer, sweeter. Sickly sweet. His frosty eyes are coated in trepidation, and I cannot get a read on the man.

"What do you want?" My anxiety was already through the roof with just being here in this new environment, now it is sky-rocketing. I wipe my sweaty palms on my shorts under the table.

William's nose wrinkles, his lips curl in distaste, his jaw tightens. He clearly doesn't like this interaction any more than I do.

So why did he sit down?

"Don't come for 4th of July." William's voice is hushed and if we weren't so close together, I wouldn't have heard him at all.

Humiliation heats my skin; I never really was one to go to parties. But to be uninvited? By a jackass like William? It hurts my pride a bit. "And what are you going to do if I show up?"

William rubs his temples and once more looks around as if he is searching for a mysterious arrival. "Just don't, *please*?" His voice is soft, desperate, as if he is trying to relay information to me that I should already know.

Before we can continue the discussion, Rayden, Maxwell's brother, walks up.

Rayden's hand lands on William's shoulder. "Well, hey there, Miss Sunday, where have you been? I have been missing you at our parties." Rayden's voice is husky and kind. Genuine. I don't know him too well, but he was nice enough when I saw him at the party.

Except I am still just as on edge as I was before. I offer up a small smile. "I haven't been up to it." I shrug a shoulder.

"Well, that's too bad. Was William inviting you to his party in a few days?" Rayden's voice is suddenly just a bit *off*.

"Actually—" I start to relay how I was in fact *un*invited, but William interrupts me.

"Yeah dude, that's what I was asking her, just like I told you. So, Sunday you better be there, or else," William says the words jokingly, but I can't help but to notice that his face is now an impenetrable mask. Emotionless.

What the fuck is going on?

Before I can really understand any of this interaction, Darius and Axel are approaching.

Axel is apparently the cook here, if the black apron covered in grease is any indication.

"Fuck off." Axel glowers at the men. Darius is holding two plates of food, but Axel's hands are free and he uses one to physically remove William from the booth.

William puts his hands up. "Look man, no problems, we were just leaving."

Rayden laughs out loud. "Aren't you on probation, wouldn't want to mess that up too, now, would you?"

I'm caught off guard by the acidity in Rayden's voice that was so gentle just moments ago, but I have to remind myself that the man Axel beat into a pulp, all those years ago, was Rayden's good friend, Mark.

Darius sets the food down in front of me and places himself between Axel and Rayden.

"Go, now, please," Darius bites out each word.

Rayden offers me one more soft grin and then the brothers a two fingered salute. "Come on Willy boy, let's go somewhere where we are welcome." Just before the door shuts behind him, Rayden calls over his shoulder, "See you at the party, Miss Sunday."

I turn my attention back to the O'Brien brothers arguing.

"You were supposed to be watching her!" Axel snaps out, I can practically see the steam coming out of his ears.

"He wasn't *supposed* to be here," Darius placates before ending the conversation altogether and sitting across from me. "Eat," he states, grabbing one plate of food.

My heart warms. In front of me is shepherd's pie. The last time I ate it was with Auggie and Tripp when we wanted to try to feed ourselves. It was the one item we thought we couldn't fuck up. We were wrong.

"Why is she leaking, you idiot?" Axel's voice startles me from the memory.

I reach up and realize that I am in fact leaking. Tears. No longer do I even notice when the emotions overflow and my waterworks release on their own. I am officially a blubbering cry baby.

"I'm sorry," I whisper out hoarsely. "I was just remembering the last time I had this." I offer up both the brothers a soft reassuring smile.

Axel is clearly still irritated, but he says nothing else as he storms off in the direction of the kitchen.

I take a bite and the flavors of the food deliver me back to that memory again. Of us laughing and throwing mashed potatoes at each other, of the shredded cheese ending up more on the counter than the food, of the decision to not eat the meat because it was undercooked.

Unlike in my memory, this food is edible. In fact it's really good.

"Did you make this?" I ask Darius.

He's mid bite and finishes it before answering. My eyes are drawn to his throat as he swallows. I avert my gaze.

"Axel did," Darius provides.

"Are all of you chefs? Must have skipped Tripp."

Darius laughs. "No, just Axel and me. We wanted to revamp this place. Make a luxury menu for the weekends, but then he got arrested, and life kept throwing punches, and we never got around to it. It does well as is, but one day, if we can make it out of this endless loop, that would be the dream."

I jerk my attention back to him, the emotion in his voice bleeds through and I can practically taste his pain. "I'm sorry." I offer up the useless words that people say, when they don't have any way of fixing something bad.

Darius chuckles again, this time he shrugs his shoulders too. "The world is a cruel place and anyone that says differently has had it lucky. But I wouldn't say they've had it easy."

His voice sharpens and I watch his face morph again, he is now a jaded older man that has gone through too much.

"Because if you live your entire life in peace, what happens when one day it all collapses? You won't have a contingency plan in place. You won't know what to do."

His words resonate.

"I think that might be me. This is the first time I feel like my bubble has popped. Like the outside world is suffocating me. On good days? I am numb and I accept just that. But on bad days? I just need to feel something besides the numbness that pushes me into the ground. I feel so buried that not even a shovel could undo the damage done. That I will live in this sinkhole until I can accept that nothing is ever going to be okay again. That this feeling, that I'm just going to have to learn to live with it. Learn to be alone." My chest is heaving as I let go of the feelings that have swirled around me for the last month.

Darius reaches out, taking my hands, his long hair swoops forward covering his soft amber eyes. "Oh, precious Wildflower, you are never going to be alone again. Not as long as any of us live and breathe. You may not know it yet, but our fates are tied intrinsically. You will forever be wrapped in our presence."

His words are heavy, *too* much. I try to tug my hands away, but his much larger ones don't allow any room to budge. His long strong fingers wrap around my wrists, shackling me.

"'Tempt not a desperate man.'" Darius suddenly releases me as if I have burned him. He stands abruptly and gathers our empty plates. "Grayson will be here soon to show you how to expo. No human interaction and think of it like a big puzzle." He rushes away and I watch until he is out of sight.

My emotions are everywhere. This rollercoaster named life has decided to take me on another loop and I'm not sure if this one will be the last or if I am stuck on this ride for the foreseeable future.

July 1st

Working, I find, is *fun* and easy. Something to focus my mind on and Darius is right–it's just a puzzle to solve. All I need to do is match the diagrams above to the plates below.

The only distraction is Axel's intense stare. He has been watching me this entire time. There is just a metal table with plates of food between us. There are two other men in the kitchen working but neither has paid me any mind.

Grayson's training consisted of pointing to the pictures and walking away.

"What is your problem?" I finally spout out after twenty more minutes of Axel's staring.

"It's just odd, how fast you already are at this."

"I'm sorry?" Did he want me to mess up so I couldn't come back? But he is right, I find myself barely even needing to look at the diagrams, I am simply relying on muscle memory, except it's only been about an hour.

He doesn't say anything else, but I feel his sharp eyes watching me as the night progresses.

"Last call!" Grayson's voice startles me out of my haze. "Take her?"

I turn around to speak to him, but he is already walking away.

It doesn't take long to see what he means. Axel is stripping off his apron. "You two got this? Want to make sure she gets home alright."

I finally acknowledge the other cooks with soft smiles. They are both older men with greying hair and round bellies. Their eyes crinkle in return.

"Sure kid." One reaches out and ruffles Axel's hair.

I find myself clenching up in anxiety, but Axel doesn't lash out, in fact he *smiles*.

"Whatever bottle you want, on Grayson." Axel laughs and half hugs both the men before stepping out from around the table and joining me. I am still in shock at what I just witnessed. He undoes my apron and places it on top of the table. He takes my hand. "Come on, Little Lamb, it's time to go." He bends down and presses the words into my ear.

Heat tingles there and everywhere he is touching. Being with Axel is the most dangerous of the brothers. He will push until I am forced into a corner. Will I lash out? Or will something else entirely different happen? My face flushes in embarrassment, but thankfully he doesn't see. He's too busy tugging me along to a back door and down the stairs.

"Sunday School."

Axel stiffens, we are at the foot of the stairs now, his motorcycle is only a few feet away.

But Maxwell is blocking our path.

"What do you want?" Axel drops my hand and bows up as if to hit Maxwell. I reach forward, unsure of what to do. I wish Darius was here.

The thought surprises me, but I push that aside. I try to pull Axel back, but he doesn't budge.

"Of course you would be with her. Just a guard dog sent out to do whichever master's bidding. How did it feel to go away for a crime you didn't commit?" Maxwell's face is all darkness and shadows. He is what I imagine as a devil in human form. I can practically see horns. Or maybe that's just his stupid gelled up hair.

Every encounter with Maxwell solidifies what I already know. He's a bad person.

But exactly *how* bad?

"What do you want?" I step carefully around Axel, trying to place myself between them, mirroring what Darius did before with Rayden.

Maxwell's lips curve up into an eerie smile. "Sunday School. We have some unfinished business, don't we?" He reaches up, but I am already jerking back.

Into Axel's arms. He wraps them around me securely, and I feel as tension leaves my body at the sanctuary of his embrace.

Axel might be filled to the brim with chaos and anger, but it's not just that. He lives in the moment, and it is contagious.

Maxwell sneers. "What's going to happen when you are out in the world again? They can't keep you under lock and key forever." Maxwell spits on the ground centimeters from my shoes. "Better watch yourself, Sunday School."

He walks briskly to his car and gets in. It squeals as he speeds out of the parking lot.

It isn't until he's gone that I realize Axel hasn't let go of me. "Axel?" I question softly. It's then that I notice we're shaking. Correction. *He's* shaking us.

"Axel?" I turn in his embrace and for the first time I see tears in his eyes.

"Please don't disappear. Please be real." The words come out heavily, saturated with a million emotions I could never even fathom to understand. "Please don't let it be like before."

"Axel?" I reach my hands up carefully, his name leaves my lips, a whisper. "What's going on? Are you okay?"

In a moment his face snaps. His tears dry. I see as he comes to some decision. "You know what? Fuck this. I don't care if you hate me for this,

I don't care what the others want, I am *done* playing by their rules. I need every moment I can have. You are the only thing that keeps me grounded in this reality."

I don't understand what he means until he is lifting me up and stepping to his bike and settling me onto it, my legs spread, my back on the handles.

He moves onto the bike facing me.

He attacks.

His lips are on mine. His hands find my waist. He rolls against me.

His hard cock presses against the thin fabric of my shorts. His hand creeps under my shirt and cups one of my breasts. His tongue licks along the seam of my lips.

Everything is on fire. He is filling all of my senses. He is imprinting into my very skin.

A hand reaches up and tugs on my hair, pulling my neck to the side. His mouth moves like a viper and latches onto the flesh there.

He sucks and licks and bites.

The feeling goes directly from my neck to the heat currently building. I clench around nothing. I want both more and less.

He has invaded me so quickly that rational thought leaves me.

We are a frenzy of emotions and wants and needs. And he knows exactly what those are and I am just meant to lay here and take it.

He pulls away from my neck like a suction popping, just like he did to my thigh. My toes curl.

His hand finds the outside of my shorts. Finds my clit through the material. He rubs a furious circle while his head falls forward pushing me further back onto the handle bars.

"Such a good Little Lamb." He nips at my ear, his furious circles on my clit not letting up.

My hips roll involuntarily into his fingers and I hear him chuckle softly.

"*Sunday*, you're fucking magnificent." He leans down and pushes my bra up under my shirt. His mouth finds one of my nipples and he plays with it with his tongue for just a moment before he is suctioning onto it and pinching my clit through my shorts.

It's too much. It is my undoing. The tension that has been building, floods my body.

I come with a breathy moan and the aftermath settles around me.

Guilt is at the forefront.

The rest rolls in; I am in public, under a restaurant.

And there are Grayson's eyes staring directly into mine as he stands at the bottom of the stairs.

For a moment I think I see something akin to lust, but quite quickly rage takes hold.

"Clean her up and take her the fuck home. I'll be there soon. Don't fuck this up," Grayson snarls out the words.

I look up to Axel, his eyes are softer than I have ever seen them before. "You okay?" he asks gently. He puts my clothes back in place as best he can, trying to rewind the evidence of the last twenty minutes.

But the wet spot visible through my shorts? The bruises I can feel forming on both my neck and breast? The flames that still lick up my spine?

He can do nothing to assuage any of that.

And what about the guilt? This is becoming a pattern. I am slowly allowing these brothers to take what should only have been Tripp's.

Axel sees my face shift. "Blame me. There is nothing to feel bad about. This was my fault. I can't keep my hands to myself. I will always love Tripp, but you? You aren't his. We promised Auggie we wouldn't touch you. Let me ask you, precious Little Lamb. Did Tripp break that promise?"

My face whitens, ice shoots through my veins. Axel knows about Tripp and me. It is clear in every word. He is mocking me.

My anger flares, I push him away and jump off the bike. I almost fall, but I catch myself at the last moment. "Just fucking take me home."

"That's a good Sunday, keep that anger. Keep that fiery rage. Because at the end of the day, all *that* really is, is *passion*."

He places the helmet on my head, and clasps the clip before getting on the bike and patting the spot behind him. I don't want to deal with Grayson, and I have zero idea where Darius is.

I begrudgingly get onto the bike. He reaches behind him and tugs me closer. I wrap my arms around his stomach. Ignoring the feel of his hard edges. The way that even after hours in the kitchen he still smells *good*. How through my guilt another feeling is beginning to fester.

I care about Axel.

About Darius.

And even about Grayson.

I just hope that that's not going to be my undoing.

He revs the bike and off we go.

July 1st

S ome days drag on longer than should be humanly possible, but we have finally made it home.

Well, to their home.

I jump off the bike and wait patiently.

"Why did you go to prison?" The question catches him off guard. The helmet he has just taken off of me falls onto the driveway. It rolls a few times before stopping in the grass.

"You don't know?" he says the words as he walks away to retrieve the helmet. "Why are you asking me anyways?"

I'm not sure why I am. But there is something about the way the question caught him entirely off guard that makes me want to know the answer even more.

"I'm a hot head, Mark did something I didn't like, and I beat his ass for it. They decided to try me as an adult. Period." He still isn't facing me. He places the helmet on his bike and starts walking to the door, he doesn't wait for me.

I jog lightly to catch up. Why is he *lying* to me? He's not even doing it well. It's as if this conversation was so unwarranted that he didn't have the time to think up an act.

I chase him up the stairs. I watch as his bedroom door swings shut, but I don't stop. I barge in.

He's somehow managed to already get his shirt off and my eyes zero in on the exposed skin.

He isn't tattooed on his chest, but it is littered with scars.

Cigarette burns. Thin white lines skittering down his chest. Two thick puckered scars across his abdomen.

I step closer and I don't think, I simply act. My hand comes up on its own accord, tracing the marks.

It is a testament to his suffering.

"What happened?"

I see indecision war on Axel's face. No longer does he remind me of Tripp in any way. This is a different man entirely. They may be twins but they have lived entirely unique lives.

Axel is a jigsaw puzzle that has been taken apart one too many times and now the puzzle is taped together. Except the pieces aren't right and the image isn't clear.

"*What happened?*" My fingers follow a long, puckered piece of skin up his abdomen, I don't stop.

"I'm a scapegoat. That is all I am good for." The words hit me in the face. My hand stutters on his chest, over his heart. It beats sharply. His large hand covers mine. His emerald eyes pierce into mine. They are open and clear. He is once more speaking without words. Willing for me to just understand.

"What do you mean?" *How did it feel to go away for a crime you didn't commit?* Maxwell's words echo around my brain.

How easy would it be to go to jail for someone else? What if that person looked exactly like you?

Tripp couldn't have. It's not possible.

My face must show the horror I am currently feeling because Axel's lips curl cruelly.

"I think you may have found your answer. I loved my brother. He had a future, a full scholarship, a *girl* he loved. I didn't have any of that." The words are laced in pain, anger, guilt. "The fucked up thing? If I hadn't done this for him, he would probably still be alive." He bends down, our hands drop, his forehead presses to mine. "But that won't change anything. What ifs are the most painful part of life. Because you know what, Sunday? Nobody actually gets a do over. They just get stuck in an endless loop of the same fucking pain. So, my suggestion to you? Enjoy every. Fucking. Moment. Because one day? You're going to look back on this instance, on every single memory, and wonder what you could have done differently. Well, I am here to tell you, humans are creatures of habit. We always end up making the same mistakes."

Another lie, another secret.

Vinegar.

That is how I feel. Exactly like vinegar.

Sour, acidic, *fermented*.

My heart is threatening to make its way outside my chest, my breath comes out in pants.

"Calm down, it's okay." Axel is both my undoing and my savior. He attempts to pull me out of the panic attack as it begins to overcome my senses.

His warmth leaves me as he goes to turn his bathtub on. He returns slowly and starts to undress me.

I don't fight him. I don't care.

He picks me up in his strong, stable, secure arms and carries me to his bathroom. The tub is almost ready.

The bathtub is clean.

He places me gently into the water. I hiss a bit as my skin grows accustomed to its heat.

"It's going to be okay, Sunday. You are going to get through this. You are stronger than you give yourself credit for."

I don't argue with him. I simply lay back and hold my breath as the water begins to fill around me.

When it covers my face entirely I pretend I can breathe.

I push my chest in and out in the façade of air.

I miss Auggie and Tripp more than I thought would be possible. I imagined every day would get a little better, but that's not how this has been going at all.

Every day is entirely different. I feel like I walk through different stages of grief and pain throughout each hour. These volatile emotions do not make sense or have any rhyme or reason. They are a beat that slowly fades to the back of my mind until something snaps it forward again. One minute I feel almost happy, but then the next I can't escape the pain of their absence.

The water ripples as I let the last of my air out.

My memory skips back to the space center. To the stairs I almost fell down. To Tripp catching me.

It jumps to the roof where we kissed, where we watched the stars, where he said he loved me.

It skitters a beat to my bedroom where I gave him every piece of myself. Where I promised I would always wait for him. Where I told him he was the only one for me.

It stutters to the present. Where I broke my promises, where I began to allow others into my heart. Because that's where Grayson, Axel, and Darius have slowly crawled into.

My heart.

I may not be in love with the men, but I care about them deeper than I wish to admit. Because the last two people I cared about so desperately?

My vision darkens and just as I lose consciousness, I feel Axel's sturdy hands tugging me up and out of the water.

July 2nd

Fuzzy. I feel fuzzy.

Everything is tumbling, moving, and spinning.

Wait, that's not right. It's me.

I try to open my eyes, but nothing changes. I am in complete darkness.

My head knocks back into a hard surface, it doesn't hurt exactly, but I use my arms to keep me in place as I continue my spiraling. My hands make contact with cool metal. I place my head on my knees, trying to keep it protected as everything continues to shake.

My fingernails drag against the material, my bare feet lodge into the bottom. I do my best to not be knocked about as whatever I am in continues its path.

I can't move my body, I am lodged in place, my knees pinned to my chest. My arms with limited mobility.

I try to discern what I'm in. I move my fingers against the surface. Up and down. Left and right.

Realization strikes me. I am inside a metal drum.

I open my mouth to scream, but nothing comes out.

Time passes in painful beats as the barrel continues its path of destruction.

Finally, after an eternity, I am stationary.

But I am no less stuck.

The urge to cry heats my eyes, but nothing comes out.

Endless emptiness shrouds me. Hopelessness finds home in my gut.

It is dark, quiet, cold, lonely.

I am scared. And every passing beat has my breath leaving a bit quicker.

Will I run out of air? Will I starve to death? Will anyone find me in time? How did I end up here?

My brain is a slushie of painful unanswerable questions.

I can feel as my panic takes hold and I begin to lose rational thought, but before I spiral too deeply, a loud noise snaps me out of it.

The lid to the barrel is removed, and I look up into soft emerald eyes. It is dark outside of the drum, but his eyes glow in the moonlight.

"Sunflower, we need to stop meeting like this." Tripp bends down and slowly, carefully tugs me out of my tomb.

We are in the woods, a tall hill stands behind us, one that is oddly familiar, past it there appears to be a large building, but it is blurry and my vision won't allow me to focus on it. Broken branches, unsettled soil, and ripped out grass prove that the hill is the path the barrel took down.

My arms reach out to grab hold of Tripp, I see that I am, but I can't physically feel it. I can't feel anything except my own inner turmoil.

I look down at my body and I see that I am in torn shorts and a stained white shirt. My feet are covered in dirt and blood. And my entire form appears to almost shimmer.

"What's wrong with me?" I sob out, but still, no tears come.

Tripp lifts me up and wraps my legs around him. "It's okay Sunflower, I've got you. We've always got you."

My head falls to the crook of his neck. After a few moments, a throat clearing has me lifting it up. Auggie stands just a couple feet away.

"Oh, lil sis. Trauma is a mysterious thing, isn't it?" Auggie steps forward and Tripp gently places me onto the ground.

I can't feel anything on my bare feet. Not the pain of the cuts digging into the ground, not the temperature, not the itchiness of the grass.

Auggie pulls me into a hug. "It's going to be okay, I promise, you just have to let it go. I love you, sis. Please just listen to me. Please," Auggie begs the word into my hair as his presence warms my heart.

I don't understand what they're saying. "I miss you two," I choke out.

Tripp steps up behind me and pulls me back into his arms. "We know Sunflower, but it's time. You need to trust my brothers. Please. Before it's too late. We can't be there for you anymore. We can only wait and hope that you won't come back here again."

My vision darkens and pain explodes across my nerves.

I open my mouth to scream.

"You knew better!" Grayson's voice is heated, angry, laced with worry.

"She is going to be fine!" Axel's deep voice throws back.

My brain is trying to catch up with this reality. I can't understand what is going on. The last I truly remember is being on the back of Axel's bike.

"You're just jealous! Just stop holding back and do what you actually want to do!" Each word Axel says is saturated in irritation.

Wait. I'm not on the bike, I'm in Axel's room. He's covered in scars. He told me he went to jail... for a crime he didn't commit. That Tripp had.

"No, I just want to be someone she can rely on while you two are thinking with your dicks," Grayson hisses the words out softly.

"Just stop it," Darius's calm voice pierces the air.

I start to shift and realize I am on a bed. The mattress is too soft to be my own and judging by the scent that surrounds me, I am in Grayson's room. In Grayson's bed.

I open my eyes.

Darius is laying next to me and he offers up a soft smile before reaching out and squeezing my hand.

The other two brothers are too heated to notice my consciousness, they are standing at the foot of the bed, staring each other down.

"Keep your distance from her before you fuck everything up." Grayson's words are threatening and he stiffens his spine, straightening up until he towers over Axel.

"Bigger men than you have tried to scare me. You aren't shit," Axel sneers.

Darius's long fingers stroke the top of my hand. "Let up, will you two?"

They both turn their wrath to him but stop when they notice I'm awake.

I offer up an unsure wave. "Hi?" I ask.

Grayson's eyes examine my face, until they stutter on my neck.

The side where Axel kissed me earlier.

"What the fuck did you do to her?" Grayson turns back to Axel, grabbing him by the shirt and lifting him against the wall. "She is eighteen! Barely an adult! She doesn't need you attacking her, confusing her!"

While I appreciate the sentiment, it also annoys me. "I'm an adult," I rasp out, sitting up.

"That's hypocritical as fuck!" Axel snarls back, wrestling against Grayson's hold.

"Let him go," Darius murmurs, his fingers tracing up my arm.

Grayson drops him, and Axel pushes against Grayson's chest.

"Until next time." Axel offers me a dirty smirk, before he storms out of the room.

Darius's hand drops and he kisses my forehead and gets up from the bed. He clasps Grayson's shoulder as he leaves the room.

"Don't," Darius warns. He turns and gives me a reassuring look before closing the door behind him.

Alone with Grayson.

An angry, red, chest heaving Grayson.

Except it doesn't make me nervous at all. Instead, I pat the bed next to me.

My gut is pulsating with energy.

Grayson lets all of the air whoosh out of his lungs before he comes over and settles next to me on the bed.

"You need to stop worrying us," Grayson states plainly. His strong hand reaches out, cupping my cheek.

I lean into the contact. "I'm an adult," I say again.

Grayson laughs and the movement has his hand pushing further into my face. His fingertips digging into my jawbone, his thumb stroking my cheek, his palm partially covering my mouth. Everywhere he touches my skin heats, it comes alive.

"You are," he agrees. His eyes catch mine. They are flickering with amusement.

I can tell he doesn't mean it, but I don't push it.

"You know from the outside looking in, you would be the bad guys in this story. Shouldn't I be running away? You all keep following me, showing up when I least expect it, manhandling me." The words muffle a bit against Grayson's hand. "And it's not just Axel, it's all of you."

"Except you trust us, don't you?" His tone is mocking.

I turn a bit and lean forward more into his hand. I am on my knees now, my face a few inches from his.

His hand on my face moves to my hair. I expect him to tuck it behind my ear, and he does, except instead of letting go, he holds onto my curls.

"You are too beautiful for your own damn good." I can tell Grayson doesn't mean to speak the words into existence. As soon as they are out, his face pales, before he slides a neutral expression into place.

For a moment his hold on my hair tightens, and I think he might kiss me but then he lets go and gently pushes me back to my side of the bed, forcing me to lie back down.

"I would tell you not to go to the river party, but no matter what I say, you aren't going to listen, are you?" Grayson's voice is resigned.

"Maybe, if you told me why I shouldn't?" I offer up as Grayson pulls the blankets over me, all the way up to my neck. His scent wafts through the space. It is unbelievably comforting, and I find that I am still incredibly tired. My eyelids grow heavy, but I want to hear his answer. I want to understand what is going on because currently I feel like a wool sack is placed firmly over my head.

Grayson lies back and wraps his arms around me. He pulls my back flat to his chest. "Can I please just hold you tonight?" Grayson's voice shakes as he speaks.

I don't argue, instead I lift the blankets and cover him with them, snuggling back closer to him. His scent, the safety of his arms, the warmth of the blankets. It isn't long before I fall asleep in his embrace.

July 4th

I am pushed against my locked bathroom door, sitting on the cool linoleum tile. The shower is running and steam is billowing into the space. My phone is in my hand, the screen slowly lighting up and coming to life.

The SIM card from the burner phone is in it.

I haven't returned to the marina to work, instead I spent the last few days recovering and back to the routine of watching movies with Darius in his room and waking up in the middle of the night to Axel. Except now Grayson is always there too. He isn't in the bed with me but resting on the ground, his attention focused on my form.

A sentinel I never asked for. A silent protector. A lonely man.

And when I wake in the morning, they're both gone.

I haven't had nearly enough time to myself, but today is the last day. I need to get any information I can before I have Carrie pick me up and kidnap me out of the O'Brien brothers' clutches.

I need to know if the dread that has burrowed itself so deeply into my skin is warranted. If the anxiety that has continued to build since Tripp and Auggie's death is leading me to something much more heinous than an accident.

Why would I need to call the sheriff about the location of the car that they *died* in?

Who better to cover up a murder than the sheriff himself? Was it for his son?

The phone is finally on. Notifications are pouring in.

There are four threads of text messages and a dozen calls in the call log.

I switch to the calls first. There's a few different numbers that I don't recognize. There's only one that I do.

Ice pierces my veins. Goosebumps pop up along my arms and legs.

Why is Julia's number on here? She isn't the last call, but a few weeks before the accident, this phone—my brother—tried to call her *several* times. She picked up for the first call, they had a short conversation, and then she wouldn't pick up again.

What is going on? That was the week she told me she would be skipping graduation and leaving town with her family on a trip. I didn't think anything at the time, but now? Is she even out of the country, or is she hiding from me? I hadn't thought to try to find her, but I also hadn't heard from her since she told me she was leaving.

She lives as far as she possibly can to still be in the city, but it seems I will be needing to make the trek to confirm if she lied to me.

My gut churns uneasily and I swallow down bile. Julia is the last person I have left, that I truly think of as a friend, but what if she was involved in my brother's death? Her sudden disappearance, which before I took as flightiness, has shifted to suspicious.

I swap to the texts.

There aren't any threads with Julia.

I click on the first one, but I don't recognize the number.

The phone clacks onto the bathroom tile as I drop it in shock. Thankfully, from my sitting position it doesn't shatter.

The message echoes around my brain. It flashes behind my eyes. My hands shake as I pick the phone back up.

My determination solidifies.

Unknown: I'M GOING TO KILL YOU

The message turns my stomach again. It's the only one on the thread.

It was sent the day before my brother and Tripp died.

Before I can think of what I am doing, I call the number. I don't know what I expect to happen, but relief pulsates through me as it goes straight to voicemail.

"The number you have called has been disconnected" comes through in a robotic voice.

My vision darkens. I try my best to carefully set the phone down and then I place my head on my knees.

Usually the position will settle me, but this time it has the opposite effect. It terrifies me.

Déjà vu slaps me in the face and I jerk to my feet.

"Sunday?" It's Darius's voice at the door.

Wrapped too fully inside my own swirling thoughts, I have no clue how long he has been there. I glance down at my phone.

There's one more thing I need to look at.

"I'll be out in a few," I promise him.

There isn't any noise to indicate his retreat, but none of the brothers have let themselves into my locked bathroom, *yet*.

I bend over and grab the fucking phone. I wish I had the ability to bury my head in the sand—as I'm beginning to suspect the O'Brien brothers are—but I don't.

I find what I am searching for.

The image gallery.

If you're going to take a polaroid, I imagine you might have gotten other photographic proof too. I brace myself.

But there was no need.

These pictures aren't of any girls in states of distress. They're of different men I recognize.

William. Maxwell. Rayden. Mark. They don't appear to be doing anything suspicious, they're all just holding cups in their hands.

The last three pictures are different.

Maxwell hands a girl a drink. Her hand is reaching up to grab it.

The yin and yang tattoo stares back at me.

The lighting is much better, but I still don't recognize the girl. She appears around my age, long chestnut hair, soft brown eyes, but with a hardened face.

Even through the picture I can tell she doesn't trust Maxwell. I wish I could scream at her, tell her to run, to trust those instincts. Based on what I can see, she appears to be wearing the same top as the night of the polaroid picture.

The next image is of William. He is handing his drink to another girl. I recognize her; she is beautiful with styled dirty blond hair, bright blue eyes, and a coy smile. She was a cheerleader in my grade. Tiffany. Maxwell's ex-girlfriend.

I flip to the last photo. This time it's of Mark. He is doing exactly what the other two men were; giving his cup to someone. Her kind smile, dark charcoal hair, and olive eyes are incredibly familiar. I grew up with her. I realize she most likely isn't guilty at all in the involvement of my brother and Tripp's death.

Julia might just be another victim.

The pictures on the phone are dated and I know with certainty it is correct. I remember Julia trying to get me to join her at this party. Her going alone. Me not hearing back from her for several days. Her shiftiness around the entire night. Eventually, I just stopped asking her about it and assumed she might have hooked up with someone. We still planned to live together in college, but our friendship had become more and more strained. It didn't help that I was carrying my own secrets about Tripp.

The party was last winter over our break.

What happened to you Julia?

"Get the fuck out here now! Or I am coming in!" Axel's voice pierces my thoughts. My suspicions.

I have just enough time to hide my phone in my bra before the door is pushing in and knocking into me.

"Get out!" I snarl the words and try to force it shut again. I am on edge and he is driving me just over the breaking point.

"I don't think I fucking will!" Axel shoves harder.

I'm not strong enough to stop him from coming inside the small room. I step back and brace myself.

He lets the door bounce against the wall as he pounces on me.

His large rough hands skate along my shorts, my pockets. He is looking for something.

I've had enough.

I jump back from him as best I can in the small space, but there he is again, invading my senses. Overwhelming me.

"Get away from me," I hiss and clench my fists.

"What are you hiding, Little Lamb?" His booming voice echoes off the linoleum. His emerald eyes darken, he bares his teeth in a snarl.

Axel lunges.

I evade him, only to trip on the shower curtain. He catches me at the last moment before I can thoroughly hurt myself. He somehow manages to roll us so that when we land in the bathtub my back is on his chest and he takes the brunt of the fall.

He lets out a garbled grunt.

I reach back and shut the water off before it can soak us any further.

I try to get off him, but he holds me in place. My ass is wedged against him. I can feel the outline of his muscles through his shirt on my back.

"Look what you did. You stupid, Little Lamb, you aren't supposed to run from the monsters," he breathes the words into my ear.

I attempt to squirm away, but one hand catches on my hip bone, the other across my chest. He restrains me as his cock hardens unmistakably against my ass.

"Yes, keep trying to escape. Do you feel what you're doing to me?" He rolls his hips up.

A wanton moan escapes my lips.

He nips at my ear. "You were made for me."

Before I can do anything else that will add to my pressing guilt and anxiety, Grayson rushes into the bathroom.

"Again?" The word leaves Grayson in both frustration and anger. He wastes no time in leaning over and wrenching me off of Axel. Grayson doesn't set me down until I am in my closet. "Change," he orders, dropping me and closing the door behind me.

July 4th

Feeling properly chastised, I rip the wet white shirt off. Thankfully my phone did not get soaked and it lights up as I remove it from my bra.

The giraffe is in the closet and I make quick work of switching the SIM cards back before changing into fresh clothes. I put a bathing suit on underneath. I need to kickstart the next step of my plan into action.

I am doing my best to keep my warring emotions at bay. I need to investigate this for myself. Tomorrow I will allow myself another meltdown, but today I need to keep my shit together.

"You're going to fuck everything up!" Grayson's shouting startles me out of my haze.

Fully dressed, I step out of the closet. Darius has joined the other two brothers. He seems to always be the voice of reason. That is further evidenced now.

Darius has a hand on each of the brother's shoulders. "Go, cool down. She and I will spend the day together." He gives me a soft smile. "Isn't that right, Wildflower?"

Grayson grumbles. He shrugs out of Darius's hand and points at his two brothers. "We promised. We can't keep doing this shit." He turns to face me and I am shocked by the way his eyes soften as they meet mine. "Please, listen to Darius today? We need you to start trusting us. Aren't we proving to you that we have the best intentions?" He gives Axel a look. "Aren't *I* proving to you that I just want what's best for you?" His voice is husky and intense. He steps to me until we are only inches apart. "Please, I'm begging you, Sunday. Don't do it. Whatever you plan on doing or wherever you plan on going. Just stay home, just tonight. Tomorrow we'll take you back to the marina, okay?" His words are wrapped in desperation, I can almost taste it as it snakes into my throat.

I swallow them down. Of everything I have done since this entire *ordeal* started, this is the only time I have felt true guilt in Grayson's presence.

Doing my best to shift my face to understanding, I look up, biting my lip. "Stay home today? You promise tomorrow I can go to the marina and leave this house? I'm going stir crazy." My voice sounds off, even to my own ears.

A dimple I hadn't noticed before forms on one of Grayson's cheeks as he offers me a half smile. He reaches up, tucking a stray curl behind my ear. His hand stays in place and his long fingers wrap around my neck. "You look like such a sweet innocent girl, and I know it's hypocritical, but I don't trust you." He applies pressure to my neck. It is just on the cusp of pain. "What can I do to convince you to believe me, to stay here?"

Uncertainty wars internally, and over Grayson's shoulder, both his brothers are watching this interaction with calculating eyes.

My eyes heat with unshed tears, not from sadness but from frustration. I am going to the river party today whether he wants me to or not, but I need to convince him I'm not. I return my attention to Grayson. I can tell the moment he sees the glassiness because his expression shifts to uncertainty. "I'm not going anywhere. I can't keep dealing with this. You all fucking know it, so I might as well say it. I was in love with your brother. I loved Tripp. Not only did my brother die, but so did my boyfriend. So did the man I thought I was going to marry."

Grayson rears back as if I had slapped him. Whatever he expected me to say, it wasn't that. But even with his reaction I can tell he *knew*. The news doesn't shock him, the surprise was that I told him.

"So, you all knew? And you talk to *me* about trust? I am living with three practical strangers! You brought me into this house where Tripp used to live. You watch my every move! For fuck's sake you won't even let me sleep alone at night. You treat me with kid gloves, as if something is going to happen to me. What is it that you aren't telling me?" By the end of my outburst I am practically screaming the words out, my hands gesticulating in the air.

Axel pushes Grayson out of the way. Grayson is apparently so shocked by my eruption he doesn't even resist. Axel takes me by the shoulders and shakes me. "You're a stupid, little girl! Of course we aren't going to tell you everything. And you loved my brother? So, what? I loved him too, but now he's gone. And the only people left that you can trust are in this fucking room. We are people, too, with feelings. And maybe if you opened your goddamn eyes, you would see that we are what you need. But no! You are a woman on a suicide mission. We know what Auggie and Tripp were up to. Sticking their noses where they shouldn't." He's snarling in my face now. His deep voice has taken on a guttural tone. "And you know what? We know that it got them killed. But what the fuck does it matter? It won't change anything. People are falsely imprisoned. It happens. A lot. And you know what that means? The guilty are never punished."

"You *know?*" The words come out a whisper, I am watching Darius closely. He is the only brother that I consider a *friend*. The only one that I was starting to truly rely on.

He averts his eyes.

Before I can discern what is happening, my hands have formed fists.

I begin hitting Axel as hard as I can on the chest. "You knew? That my brother was murdered? That Tripp was murdered?"

"Stop her," Darius murmurs the words. "Before she hurts herself."

I cackle a laugh taken straight from the insanity of this moment. My heart pulsates. I can see red. But it's not in anger. The red is crimson blood. It soaks into this moment.

Betrayal.

Axel catches my next punch, but I don't let it stop me. I use a leg and start kicking at his shin. "You are right! You are a fucking monster. How could you? And you knew that I loved him? How could you all?" I don't realize that I am sobbing until my vision blurs. "You kissed me... you.... Why would you?" I lose my fight. My cries escape in painful hiccups.

Axel reaches for me, but I step back until I am flat against the closet door. A cornered animal. The prey. The Little Lamb he calls me.

Shame burrows into my stomach.

"I should have gone to my grandmother's."

"We can't keep you safe there." Grayson's monotone words slice through my emotional turmoil.

"That. Isn't. Your. Job," I clip the words out. "You all can fuck off. I may be stuck in this house, but I am through with you following me around. Of your overbearing nature. I will go back to work tomorrow at the marina, but tonight? I am going to do whatever the fuck I want." Instead of feeling the hurt by their betrayal I allow the fury to seep into my veins. It is keeping me from breaking down again.

"It isn't safe." Darius's voice is calm, placating. He tries to hide it, but I can hear the hitch of panic in the middle.

"I don't care. Unless you have some answers or there is anything else you want to tell me?"

The three brothers all look to each other.

"I didn't think so. Well listen to me fucking carefully–" I inhale a deep breath, wipe away my tears, and square my shoulders "–if I see any of you at the party, I am going to leave and I am never coming back. I will convince my parents to let me stay alone or I will suck it up and stay with my grandmother for the foreseeable future." It's a bluff... partially. I plan on sticking around until those guilty get the karma they deserve.

I don't wait for their answer. My phone is on my person and that is all I need. I push past Axel, I try to step around Darius but he extends his arm, blocking the doorway.

If it weren't for the concern written plainly in his flat lips and furrowed brow, I would have ignored him entirely.

"It isn't safe. I know you are looking for clues or whatever fucked thing you are wanting to find, but please, at the very least, let me come with?"

"You won't stop me?" I question accusatorily.

His throat bobs as he swallows thickly. "Not unless—"

"There is no 'unless.'" I pull free, but he catches me again.

"I won't stop you," he promises this time.

"Fine." Even with this revelation, I need him more than I care to admit. I need his support, his calming aura. He makes me feel like everything is going to be okay. "But you follow my lead. And they–" I jerk my head towards Axel and Grayson "–aren't coming."

"Wait, hold the fuck on." Axel's tone is heated.

"Agreed," Darius says firmly. "You two will stay clear. Got it?"

"No," Axel argues. "She can't just throw a fucking tantrum and we listen to her."

"This is your fault. *Again*." Grayson's face is resolved. He lets the air out of his lungs in a long shaky exhale. "Be safe?" He grabs Axel's shoulders, holding him in place. "Go." The word is a whisper.

Darius nods once before he pulls us out the room. "Text your ride."

"How do you—" I don't bother finishing the question. I know what was disclosed earlier is the last of the information the O'Brien brothers will be divulging to me for quite some time. I pull out my phone and shoot Carrie a text that I no longer need a ride. I don't wait for a response before tucking it back into my pocket.

We are halfway to the front door now and my eyes catch on the picture of Axel and Tripp that I spotted the first day here. I stutter to a stop, even as Darius tries to yank me forward.

"I had it wrong." I had never mistaken the twins before, except for this picture. I thought I knew who Tripp and Axel were with certainty, but looking at it now? "How did they change so much?" The sweet soft twin looking back at me I can now clearly tell is Axel. It is in the way he stands, even as a child. It is the weight of his eyes, the surety of his stance, the slope of his shoulders. Meanwhile, Tripp is frowning, staring at something over the camera, he looks annoyed and like he's ready to run off as soon as he can.

Darius is watching me, but he doesn't say anything. He just allows me a few more moments to process before he is tugging me again, this time gently. "Come on, we need to go before Axel loses it."

"What happened to him? Why is he so different? Was it just his time in prison?" I don't know why I am asking. Why I even care. Actually I do, but I am going to continue to lie to myself.

Axel has gotten under my skin.

Darius doesn't bother answering, instead he drags me until we are through the garage door. There are three vehicles; his truck, Grayson's car, and Axel's motorcycle.

A childish part of me wants to kick over Axel's motorcycle, but I refrain. I should be equally mad at all three brother's, but for some reason I thought Axel wouldn't bullshit me.

I hop into the truck. Darius gives me one long, hard look.

"Drive," I demand. I cross my arms and stare pointedly away.

He does.

July 4th

After a long and silent ride, we make it to our destination. A patch of gravel a few hundred feet from the riverbank and near William's house. Even from the distance I can see there is a large crowd at the water.

I turn to Darius. "Is there anything else you want to tell me about this? How do you all know? Do you know who it was?" The questions roll out one after another.

Darius places his forehead onto the steering wheel. He turns his head to face me. He pauses for a few moments just staring at me. I can see the moment he decides to speak.

He sighs dramatically. "Tripp told us." His face is sad, washed in pain.

Once more, I have forgotten that I am not the only one suffering, but I am selfish and, in this moment, I am too angry to care.

"We don't know who it was. We just know that some fucked shit was going on." Darius sits up and his eyes stare past me down to the party. "But we have our suspicions. The men we are trying to keep you away from."

"What about the girls?" The words break as they leave my lips. I don't want to speak the evil that befell them into existence, but the truth of the matter is I am scared to. "They were rap—"

Darius's sharp eyes flicker to mine. "So you are figuring everything out." His tone feels scolding.

I frown. "And you're okay with how ever many more countless victims there will be?"

"No." He unbuckles his seatbelt and leaps across the cab at me. He's in my face. "But I can't help them. They aren't my priority. I want to keep *you* protected."

He speaks the words against my lips. His large hands come up to cup my cheeks. His rough fingers stroke my skin. He's lighting me on fire.

I can't tell if the flames are demanding me to fuck or fight.

"I wish I could save every girl from every horrendous thing the world has in store, but I can't. There is only one person I plan on keeping safe and that's you."

He pushes his soft lips to mine. Before I realize what he has done, he is pulling away and if it weren't for the heat he left in his wake, I might think I imagined it.

I bring my hands up and push against his chest. As soon as the brothers invade my space my brain goes to mush. But I'm livid, I won't let him distract me. They betrayed me. I need to remember that.

"My only friend left might have been hurt by these disgusting men. Mark, Maxwell, William. They're all guilty."

"So, what?" Darius shouts the words causing me to jump back. I've never heard him this loud before, not even when I leapt out his truck in the middle of the road. "So, what if they're guilty? Axel is right. Nothing is ever going to change. Tripp tried his way and all that happened was I lost one brother for years; Axel is never going to get over whatever the fuck he went through. And he wouldn't tell any of us. Tripp wouldn't let it go and he tried again and now he's dead. Now your brother is dead. And if you aren't careful, you're going to join them too!" Darius pants out the last word. His chest heaves with the exertion of his anger.

"I don't care." I am being a brat, but I mean it. Ripping my seatbelt off, I jump out of the truck before he can stop me. I know I'm not being rational, but they *lied* to me.

I want to break down and bury myself in my pain. Instead, I push my energy into something else.

I don't look back at Darius even as I hear him get out of the truck, I simply walk my way to the party goers.

As I approach, I see Maxwell, William, and Mark sitting in the water passing a joint between them. I keep my attention on the interaction.

One of those men murdered Auggie and Tripp, and I am going to find out who.

July 4th

"**S**unday!" Carrie's voice snaps me out of my anger. It is pitched just a bit too loud. She comes charging from the river, covered in water, and launches herself at me.

"Hi, Carrie." I pat her gently on the back. Even with her face buried in my shoulder I can smell the alcohol coming off her. I am suddenly incredibly grateful Darius decided to join me. How was she planning on getting me in this state? "You good?"

"Yes!! I have been thinking bout you." She draws the words out as she pulls away from me.

I shiver as a gust of wind whips out at my now damp clothes.

With Carrie no longer pressed against me, I can see her. It hasn't been more than a few weeks, but she doesn't look good. Her eyes are bloodshot, her cheeks sunken in, her nose raw and red.

"Are you sure?" I whisper the words out softly. I need to tell her about Maxwell, warn her away from him, but I'm beginning to suspect she isn't with him by choice. I don't know what to do. It's hard to have the emotional capacity for others when I don't even have it for myself.

She furrows her eyebrows and annoyance whips across her face.

She doesn't have the chance to say anything prior to the devil himself approaching.

"Sunday School." Maxwell's lips curl up into a taunting smile. He wraps an aggressive arm around Carrie's shoulders. I watch as she tries to evade his touch. His eyes look past me. "Only one bodyguard today?" he asks maliciously.

I ignore him, focusing on Carrie. "I can help."

For a moment I see something deep and painful float through Carrie, almost as if she might just talk to me, but then Maxwell squeezes her shoulder.

"I've got to go! Time for shots!" She offers up a plastic smile and tries to escape Maxwell's imprisonment. I can see the moment he allows her, but red claw marks are left in his wake.

Someone steps in behind me. His smell is familiar and safe.

"Maxwell." Darius places his large comforting hands gently on my shoulders and rests his chin on my head. "We were just going to hop in the river before we lose the rest of this sunlight."

Maxwell flares his nostrils, but before this can escalate, Rayden walks up. "Lay off brother, let them have a good time." Rayden offers me a kind grin. "How you been, Miss Sunday? So glad you could make it."

Darius's strong fingers press into my shoulder bones. I don't think he realizes he's doing it. I reach up and cup one of his hands gently and the pressure lightens.

Irritation flashes across Maxwell's face, but something else entirely lights up Rayden's. I can't tell what it is, but it sends another shiver down my spine. This time it isn't from the wind.

Rayden hasn't given me any reason to mistrust him, but he was in a picture on the phone my brother had. Grayson told me to steer clear of him. He is Maxwell's brother. He is a Thorne.

Veronica comes to join our foray. I offer her my first genuine smile since getting here.

She doesn't wait for anyone, she simply snags me from Darius's hold and walks me to the river. I give him one backwards worried look, but he lifts his lips reassuringly.

"You looked like you could use an escape route," Veronica explains. She strips out of her clothes to her bathing suit and I do the same, throwing them in a pile on the ground.

I try to look for Carrie, but I don't see her.

Veronica watches me closely as we step into the river. Scrutinizing me. My reactions.

I hiss at the frigid water, but after a few moments, I grow accustomed to it and take a few more steps before sitting down. The rocks dig into my skin and I absentmindedly begin to play with them.

Veronica crosses her legs and lowers herself carefully beside me. She has somehow secured two beers in the few moments I turned away.

I watch her open both and she offers me one.

I don't really want it, but I also don't want to tell her no.

"I miss them both," Veronica states after a few more moments of silence. Her voice is *off*. Ladened in guilt. Something has changed since the last time we spoke. "Dating your brother meant I was around Tripp more than I wanted to be." She whips her hair back and rolls her lips between her teeth. "He wouldn't shut up about you."

"Auggie?" I'm watching her carefully as I sip the beer. I dig my hand into the sediment below, but the feeling on my skin causes a bolt of panic to shoot down my nerves.

I gasp in surprise and Veronica arches a brow and comments, "Tripp. That fucker loved you. Everyone knew it except Auggie. Well, maybe even he did." Veronica laughs, but there's no humor in it. "William isn't like the others, you know?"

The words catch me off guard and I choke on my sip of beer, spluttering for a moment. "What do you mean?" I feign ignorance.

She cackles. "You have no poker face Sunday." She pushes her shoulder into mine. "You don't have to believe me. You know this world, this town especially, is full of evil men. I've learned even more about it recently." Her eyes close, her teeth draw blood from her bottom lip. She offers me a crimson smile. "He does what he has to. He keeps me safe." She licks the liquid away before it can roll down her face. "Your brother did what he could to keep you safe and mine did the same."

Safe. Safe. Safe.

But from what?

A thought strikes me. "Why weren't you in the car with my brother and Tripp, Veronica?" The words come out a hoarse whisper. My skin prickles with goosebumps, my heart begins to pound against my chest.

Veronica's face goes white, her hand on the beer shakes, she bites down on her already bloody lip even harder. "Sunday. I care about you. I want the best for you. But this town is owned by a powerful family. The world is a woven tapestry of mistakes and choices. We never know what each day will bring, what our decisions can lead to. We can only guess. We can only hope that everything works out as best it can." Her glassy eyes meet mine. "I didn't know. I'm sorry," she rasps the words out before standing abruptly, she turns back one last time and I can see the blood from her lip has fallen to her chin now. She's a ghost. A person that should have been with Tripp and Auggie when they died. A living apparition. "If you ever need me, I am going to be your Auggie." She wipes her face and states the words with finality before joining the party goers on the shore.

I lose myself to my thoughts. This day has unraveled more than I expected. If I focus on all the pieces of the torn up puzzle, I don't have to look at the shape. I don't have to see that everyone in this town knew my brother and Tripp were murdered before I did. Because that's what she said wasn't it? William knew what was going to happen. He kept her from being with them.

"Leave her alone." William is the last person I want to see, but here he is, taking Veronica's place next to me.

"Leave *me* alone," I respond firmly.

He gets really close until his disgusting breath is in my ear. "I told you not to come. I am doing what I can, but I can't keep you safe, too. You need to leave, but it might already be too late."

Before I can really grasp what he is saying, he shoves me forward into the water, knocking the beer from my hand, and I screech in surprise.

He laughs severely before stomping away. I try to find the bottle, but the river has taken it. Swept it away.

I push myself up and get to my feet only to see that half the party is staring at me now.

The thirty or so eyes feel like thousands. As if I am an insect being examined under a microscope.

I need to get away, I can't breathe. I find myself looking for Darius, but I don't see him. I start splashing my way down the river instead.

The sun is setting. When it is dark enough, I will return, but right now I need to calm my nerves. To process the overwhelming dump of knowledge that has been thrown my way today.

And buried at the very bottom of that is the painful realization of how alone I am. That my parents haven't reached out once since they left me to deal with the aftermath of their favorite child's death. That the only people I have left to rely on are the O'Briens and they lied to me. They knew Tripp and Auggie were murdered, and they didn't even tell me, but instead of anger all I feel is a weighted sadness.

I continue my journey. The river has stayed shallow and calm through my walk, but as I continue, a disturbing feeling slithers up the back of my neck, prickling the skin. As if I am being watched. I whip around, but I don't see anyone. The partygoers are once more drinking and mingling on the water's edge, but they are now quite a distance away. I am right at the river's bend and soon I will be out of their sight.

I make the turn and a few more steps in, I freeze.

Everything is incredibly, eerily silent. The trees block any of the remaining sunlight and I am completely in shadows. And even more so? The unsettling feeling of déjà vu. This time it's accompanied by a scene that flashes to mind. Both familiar and unfamiliar. I don't have the chance to register what it is before it disappears and I am standing back in this moment.

But it leaves me terrified, on edge.

My instincts are screaming *I should not be here*. Across the river on the bank, I swear I see movement. Nothing has happened, but I know I should scream. I go to do just that but a hand wraps over my mouth.

"Hush it's just me, but we need to go. Now." Grayson's lips brush my ear as he speaks.

"I thought—"

"You can be angry with me later." He begins pulling me back the way we came. The river splashes loudly as we take large steps.

Behind us, there's noise, but I don't look back. I don't want to fall.

"It's going to be okay." I can barely hear him over the sound of our retreat.

What are we running from? *Who* are we running from?

When we are a bit closer to the party, Grayson drags us to the shore.

"I'm not done here," I say firmly, even as terror courses through me.

"I figured as much, you stubborn girl." His long fingers wrap around my wrist and we slowly make our way along the riverbank to the party. I try to look back from where we came, but I can't see anything.

"What was *that*?" I don't bother to ask why he's here. I have quickly realized the men are tethered to me. Once again, I am grateful for it.

Rayden, William, Maxwell, and Mark are all notably absent from the party when we finally make our way back.

I stop where my clothes lay, Veronica's no longer with them. I pull from Grayson to tug them on and the motion catches his attention.

His eyes stutter on my chest. He gulps and glances away abruptly. "Put some fucking clothes on." He closes his eyes and rubs his temples. "Please," he adds begrudgingly.

"That's what I'm doing." I don't argue further. My heart is still racing, my nerves pumping with adrenaline as I slip my clothes on over my mostly dry swim suit. "Where's Darius?"

Grayson heaves out a heavy sigh. "Occupied."

We are two of the last people at the river, most have made their way up the hill to William's house. In the opposite direction is where we parked. Darius's truck is still there.

"Is he... okay?" My voice is suddenly unsure. The eldest O'Brien brother makes me feel the most small, inadequate, naïve. But I also feel safe with him. Just like I do with all of them.

I watch his face. A wrinkle has formed between his eyebrows. He is difficult to read. But after a moment, I recognize the emotion–it's one that I have carried with me since the day of the memorial.

Apprehension.

"Fuck." He expels the word and gestures to the house. "Let's go. Lead the way. Axel is with Darius. He's going to be okay. He shouldn't have agreed to this. It isn't safe. I just want to keep you all alive." His voice softens as the words progress.

I'm a dog with a bone. A curious cat.

A stupid broken girl.

I know that this isn't a good idea, but I can't help it. A spark of worry twists in my gut about Darius. About whatever the fuck that was on the river, but I ignore it. I stamp it down. This is one chance I most likely won't have again. I don't plan on coming back here.

He captures my hand, laces our fingers, and without further ado, I guide us to wherever my unrelenting mind commands.

July 4th

I lead us through an unlocked side door of the huge house. It appears to be a mud room. I have an idea of what I'm looking for.

There aren't any party goers on this side, but I can hear the base of a DJ, the sound of laughter, and the repeated chanting of the word "chug." For a moment I wish I could be one of them and just pretend everything is okay. That there isn't something incredibly dark in this town.

"Sunday?" Grayson murmurs gently, squeezing my hand. "Please, baby girl. Do your search, but we need to hurry. I don't want to get caught. We don't have a lot of time." His urgency propels me into gear.

The mud room has two doors.

The left one leads to the main part of the house, but the right one leads to a garage.

The garage is exactly where I want to go.

Stepping into the huge space, I slowly shut the door behind us and use the flood lights to search the area. There is a refrigerator, a long tool bench, and a set of weights. The space is enough for six cars and each spot is taken. Four of the vehicles are covered in tarps and two are not.

Surely, they didn't?

"Baby girl, are you sure? There's no turning back. This is going to be dangerous. Not just for you." Grayson's gentle voice is a stark contrast to his words. They are harsh. They pierce my resolve and I falter.

"Not just for me." The words leave my lips before I can take them back. He's right. I look at Grayson. Fully take him in. Once more, I need to remind myself that he is doing what he thinks is best. He's trying to protect his two remaining brothers. He doesn't want the same fate to befall them as it did Tripp.

My determination wavers. What if they end up dead because of me? What if instead of bringing forth justice I cause just another tragedy.

A voice outside the garage door splinters my thoughts.

"Come on, no one's out here." It's Mark.

"Already?" I can barely discern the word from Grayson before I make a quick decision. I rush us under the tarp of the nearest vehicle.

We have just enough time to press our backs against the car before the door we came through earlier opens again. Leaning further back I have to physically stop myself from yelping in pain. The metal of the car isn't smooth, it is jagged. It tears through my shirt into my skin.

"Mark," the voice whines. "I need to go back to Maxwell."

"Shut up, slut, get on your knees. You know you like this shit."

"No," her voice wobbles.

My heart is breaking. I don't know if I can stay here if Mark decides to do anything else. I have a grasp of what these men are capable of.

It isn't anything good.

And that girl he has with him?

It's Carrie.

"Mark? Get your ass back here. We have a church girl to find." Maxwell's slimy voice permeates the room.

I can't see anything, but I can hear as Mark lugs Carrie with him out of the room.

I move to leave the tarp, but when I do I catch a glimpse of the vehicle beneath.

Grayson's hand finds its place over my mouth before the scream pierces the air.

"Hush, it's okay. Can we go home now please?" he begs me.

I nod my head softly. I can't do anything. I am a useless teenage girl that is about to get the only people in her life killed.

The brothers told me I shouldn't come here. I'm not sure if they already knew Auggie's destroyed car would be here. Or if they just guessed. But the sight of it has the day's events catching up to me in quick procession.

I wrench away from Grayson and step to the car. I run my fingers along the scratches.

The black paint color is familiar. It's not normal black. It's an even darker shade that brings one specific vehicle to mind.

Maxwell's BMW.

"We need to go." Grayson's voice is urgent. Saturated in paranoia.

He grabs my hand. I expect to go through the house again, but he pulls us to the wall.

"When the garage door opens, you run to the headlights of Darius's truck and you don't look back."

"But—"

"Baby girl. I need you to listen to me. I know none of this makes sense, but you have to listen. Please."

"But—"

He does the last thing I expect. He presses his lips to mine to shut me up. The kiss is fast, hot, searing. He tears away and pushes me to the garage door.

"Now!" He presses the button, but he doesn't move.

I am so in shock by the kiss that I listen to him. As soon as there's enough space I sprint as fast as my bare feet can take me. Darius' truck is now parked as close as he can be to the house, between the trees. When I make it to the vehicle, I look back expecting Grayson but he isn't there.

I want to return, but I don't have time to. A set of arms scoops me from behind and throws me into the bed of the truck. The person—Axel—jumps in after banging the window. "We have to leave him. Go!"

"Wait, what? What do you mean *leave him*?" My voice is shrill.

The truck jerks us out of the gravel drive and down a long driveway.

"You, stupid little girl! Why can't you just listen to us?" Axel's anger is hot as he whips the words at me harder than the wind.

Darius is now speeding away and I am abjectly aware of my lack of clothes, the darkness, and the painful breeze slapping me.

I begin to shiver and my teeth clatter as we make it onto the main road.

I focus my attention on the stars above. The one constant in my life.

Axel moves beside me, he goes to wrap his leather jacket around me, but his fingers find the scratch on my back. "You find what you were looking for?" His tone is mocking.

I deserve it. I don't say anything and he leans against the back of the truck, pulling me carefully to his side. Enveloping me in his scent and warmth. I don't deserve it.

"I'm sorry." The words come out hoarsely. "You're right. I shouldn't have gone."

Axel doesn't acknowledge my words except to squeeze me tighter into his side. "They know Auggie was onto them. We don't know who it was. Or if it was all of them. They know about the phone. They know you probably have it. They were testing a theory, if you were onto them. If you were going to follow the same path Tripp and Auggie did. If you need to be *dealt* with like they were. You fell hook, line, and sinker," he pushes the words into my ear.

I try to lean up to do the same, but I can't reach. A bump on the road has me bouncing off the cab floor, but he catches me and I land in his lap. He wraps his arms around me and he rests his sharp chin on my shoulder.

"How do you know?" I try to shoot the words so that they won't get lost to the noises around us.

"Because I know bad men. They make traps and lead Little Lambs there. Let me ask you, have they been putting Carrie in your view more? Try to lure you out with her?"

I nod slowly.

"Grayson is going to be okay, but you can't do this again. You have to trust us. We don't know everything, we're just guessing, but Tripp and Auggie told me enough. And I know why Tripp beat Mark's ass in the first place. But this town is owned and ruled by the Thornes. You need to remember that." He squeezes me tighter.

I'm not sure if it's the adrenaline of the day, the terror, the security of Axel's arms, or the stars shining comfortingly above, but eventually, my eyelids grow heavy.

As I float off into nothingness, I hear Axel humming a familiar tune from my childhood.

July 5th

I shoot up off the bed I am on. My hands find the material below me and I squeeze onto the soft sheets. My eyes blink rapidly as I try to gain my bearings.

"Good morning." Darius's voice cuts through my confusion.

I turn my head, and there he is, leaning against my bedroom door, sitting on the ground exactly where Grayson usually is.

Axel isn't in my room, just Darius. The realization leaves me anxious. Off-kilter. I can tell something isn't right.

I meet Darius's eyes and my breath stutters. His left one is practically swollen shut black and blue, his cheek purpling, his lip split. I observe the rest of him. His knuckles are scabbed, a bandage is over his forearm.

"What happened?" Dread and guilt layer themselves up my throat until I can hardly breathe.

"It isn't your fault. I need you to understand that what these men do, it is on them alone."

A memory seeps through. "Where is Grayson?"

Darius cringes and slowly carefully lifts himself off the ground. He tries to hide it but I can see the slight limp as he approaches. "He's going to be okay." Darius's voice is matter-of-fact, holding no emotion.

He lays gently down next to me, tugging me to his side.

"It would have happened eventually. We needed to be 'taught' a lesson. The Thornes own this town."

Mulling over his words, I turn on the bed and carefully trace the line of his split lip.

Darius leans into my touch.

"Where's Grayson? Please. Stop hiding things from me."

Darius recoils but remains silent for a few more moments. His attention is focused firmly out the window.

The blinds are pulled back, it's dark outside, but I can tell the sun is on its way up.

He finally comes to some decision and returns his attention to me. "He's in the hospital."

I gasp and my fingers stutter on the corner of his mouth.

"Come here." He gently moves me up and onto his lap so that I am straddling him.

I try to escape. "I'm going to hurt you."

"You won't." His hands find the backs of my thighs. His calloused fingers stroke the exposed skin leaving prickles in their wake.

I carefully place my hands on his solid shoulders. Warmth courses through my veins.

I watch his face. I imagine if I were to look in a mirror the same emotions would be reflected.

Worry. Want. Concern. Lust.

Love?

I'm sorry, Tripp.

I lean over until my wild curls fall forward. I watch Darius as slowly, ever so carefully, I press my lips to his.

I can tell he is shocked but then the fingers on my thighs squeeze. He presses me as tightly to him as he can. My tongue licks carefully along his lips. He groans, the vibrations causing heat to furl deep in my belly.

The kiss starts slow, languid, calm. But then I nibble gently on his bottom injured lip.

It ignites him.

Before I can grasp what is happening, he has us flipped. His knees between my thighs. One hand catches in my hair, yanking my head exactly how he wants me, the other one reaches above us holding himself from crushing me with his weight.

He pulls back. "Wildflower. I need you."

He ignores his injuries completely as he reclaims my lips, consuming me.

The kiss deepens. His tongue clashes with mine, the metal piercing hitting my teeth with a clink. He grips my hair so tightly it is just on the cusp of pain.

I moan softly into his mouth, rolling my hips upwards. I need the friction. Something. Anything. I can feel the hardness of his cock. My core throbs. My body is demanding more. I *want* more.

Finally, when stars begin darting behind my eyelids he separates from me. He leaves me a breathless panting mess. He has scorched me, touching spots inside my heart that I thought were walled off.

As if reading my mind, Darius releases my lips. "Can I taste you?"

His question throws me off, but in this moment, I take a page from Axel. I don't think, I just live in the moment and agree, "Yes."

The one word is all it takes. I watch Darius transform before my eyes. He is no longer the friend that he has been, he is a predator, the storm, a hurricane. "I have something I want to try. Do you trust me?"

I realize with certainty, that even with what they hid from me, I completely trust Darius. He has done everything to be there for me, to keep me safe. "I do," I murmur the words, looking up at him through my lashes.

"Good." He leans back up and reaches into his pocket for something, for a moment I think it's going to be a condom, but then he pulls out something metal. "I think you'll like this."

My attention shifts when he abruptly yanks my shorts down, and I look up just in time to see him putting something back into his pocket.

He shifts down the bed and flashes me his tongue. There is a larger metal part on it now. I am not quite sure what he has done until he finds his way to the apex of my thighs. Until his tongue makes it to my clit.

His *vibrating* tongue.

"Holy *fuck,*" I expel in a breathy whimper as shockwaves ripple across my nerves in thick long waves.

He pulls back for a moment and offers me a cheeky smile. "I thought you might like this."

He doesn't give me a chance to question why he had this on him as his tongue returns to my clit and I am once more at his mercy.

"Fuck, fuck, *fuck.*" I don't even need anything else. His tongue is making quick work of bringing me to the edge faster than I have ever gone.

He pauses for a moment and it is almost enough to let the guilt of what I am doing burst its way through before his long fingers are pushing into me, one at first in soft steady thrusts. Once I adjust, he adds another.

"Darius," I plead. I crave more and less of him at the same time. My hands find the mattress below, my fingers curling into the sheets.

He moves his tongue. Coupled with the vibrations, it's a new sensation that I have never felt before, but I fucking love it. So much so, that I would do anything in this moment for him to never stop. I am shuddering against the mattress unconsciously arching up into him while my hands keep me latched to the mattress.

His two fingers curl at a spot just inside that causes me to quiver.

"Darius, please," I pant the words out. I don't know what I am begging for, but he seems to understand.

His fingers begin to frantically pound a beat as they curl into the same spot just inside over and over again. He hums against my clit as his tongue and the piercing work me over.

I hit the breaking point as the pressure inside surges upwards and out.

The scream that leaves my body is a surprise second only to the excess wetness that rushes out of me.

"I—I—" I am suddenly unsure of what just happened. It felt amazing, but I had never felt exactly like *that* before.

Darius leans back on his heels and wipes his face. His *very* wet face. Darius's lips curl in satisfaction as he finds my attention on him.

"You squirted," Darius tells me.

"I'm sorry." Embarrassment is now wrapping up my stomach.

He shifts up the bed until he is once more hovering over me. I try to turn my head on the mattress, but he grips my chin, forcing me to look him in the eyes. "Do not ever apologize, you are the sexiest woman I have ever met and being able to make you do that? That's the biggest compliment I could ever receive."

Once more Darius is reassuring me and making every encounter a safe and comfortable experience.

Darius is stamping himself into my life. Into my very being. Existential dread drops like an iron down my throat. I try to swallow around it.

"Darius," I rasp the word out. "Please don't leave me." Terror suddenly strikes, causing my heart to beat rapidly. I'm inexplicably afraid that if this moment ends, I won't see him again.

My hands reach up to gently trace his bruised cheek. He leans into the touch, pushing down until I can feel his heart beating against mine.

A muffled noise sounds. It's his phone ringing.

"I'm not the one that keeps running away." He offers a bitter grin before kissing the tip of my nose and rolling carefully off of me.

This time he mutters in pain at the movement. He yanks his phone out of his pocket, answering it.

"Update? Is it time?" Darius barks the words into the phone.

A pause, he glances at me.

"Fuck off. I'm bringing her. You're a fucking idiot," he barks out in a harsh rasp.

He moves the phone to his shoulder and offers me his hands. I carefully take them and he tugs me up.

"We'll be there in an hour." He pushes me to the bathroom. "I know I was wrong. That doesn't help anything," he says into the phone as he closes me inside the bathroom door. I try to listen for the rest of the conversation, but I can't hear it.

Now that I am no longer in the moment with Darius, my mind is slowly processing the last day of events. Crippling depression and guilt trickle into me.

Auggie and Tripp were murdered.

There is something evil being hidden in plain sight in this town.

Carrie isn't okay. Julia isn't okay.

Darius and Grayson were hurt because of me.

Veronica knows more than she is letting on.

The sheriff has Auggie's car.

The totaled car looked like it had been hit by Maxwell's BMW.

I stare at my reflection in the mirror.

My copper curls are a wild mess, my stormy eyes are sunken and hollow, my lips are dull. I feel like I am slowly fading from existence.

I want to find out who killed Auggie and Tripp, but what about the living O'Briens?

I pull my hands back, I want to break, hurt, destroy.

"Wildflower!" Darius's stern voice breaks through the silence.

Fuck.

I jerk away from the mirror. I can't stand to look at myself. All I am doing is causing more harm.

I turn on the shower.

July 5th

The hospital smells of death, decay, and bleach. My nose wrinkles as the doors shut behind us with a snap. We walk in, and I find myself pointedly ignoring the full waiting room.

I am suddenly aware of how little contact I have had with the outside world, and the loud room is off-putting.

"Come on," Darius coaxes me with his soft calm voice. He's back to being my friend and I appreciate it. He seems to already know where we are going and leads me up an elevator, through several hallways, until we make it to the outside of a door to a hospital room.

He turns to me.

"He's going to look worse than it is, okay? And I need you to remember that no matter what happened, it isn't your fault."

"Whose fault is it then?" My voice breaks as it weakly leaves my lips.

Darius's eyes find mine. I try to look away, but his large hand reaches up, he pinches my chin between his thumb and finger. "It is the men who hurt him. It is the Thornes, their lackeys, and every other person that was involved. You were not the cause. This was inevitable. They just chose to act because he was there."

Anxiety flushes through me. It has the weight of a thousand cars. The depth of an endless chasm. The feel of being shaken in a barrel, unable to move.

What? The last thought feels too *real*.

Why does everything hurt so much?

I don't realize I'm trembling until Darius reaches forward and pulls me into his chest.

"It's okay, everything is going to be alright." The words don't soothe me, but his voice does.

Embarrassment heats my cheeks at my public display, I look up from his shoulder, but the hallway we are standing in is empty. I extract myself from his refuge.

"I'm ready."

I can tell he doesn't believe me, but he opens the door nonetheless.

I'm *not* ready.

My gasp is inaudible over the noise of the hospital equipment.

Grayson isn't okay. Grayson is wrapped from head to toe in something or another.

He isn't awake. He's hooked up to a ventilator. The steady beep strums at my nerves and each time, it pierces a bit further into my heart.

Grayson was the O'Brien I looked up to. The one I thought no harm could come to. The one that was there when I needed him the most. He was indestructible.

Except he's not.

Everyone I care about is going to leave me. Or die.

This time I can't help the flood of tears. I am so incredibly overwhelmed by the sight that I don't see Axel until he is standing up from a chair next to Grayson's side.

"I told you not to bring her," Axel grunts out harshly to Darius, before taking me in his arms. "Come here, I've got you, Little Lamb. That's a good Sunday, come here and breathe." He resituates us in the chair, placing me in his lap.

This close I can see the rise and fall of Grayson's chest. The only physical indicator that the man is still alive. That the world hasn't lost another O'Brien.

"Did you call your mom?" I'm not sure why that is the question I decide to ask, but I wish I can take it back when Axel stiffens underneath me.

"The *oven* doesn't need to know. We have each other. I doubt she would come anyway," Axel rumbles the words into my ear. He tickles the skin and I involuntarily shiver.

My hand carefully moves forward. The blanket covers most of Grayson, but his hand closest to us is exposed. I reach for it.

The size difference is almost comical as I place mine in his, squeezing.

I want to pretend I feel his hand move, but I don't.

"What if he doesn't wake up?" This time when the words slip out it's me stiffening.

Axel doesn't even react.

Darius drags a chair up next to us sitting down. "He will." Darius sounds surer than he has any right to.

"How do you know?" I wish I could shut up, but I can't.

Axel chuckles in my ear. "Because how will he chew us all out if he doesn't wake up? He knew what going there meant."

"How did he end up here, in the hospital?"

The room's door opens again and I jerk my attention to it, dropping Grayson's hand.

"That would be me."

July 5th

"Veronica?" I'm not sure who I expect to see, but it's not her.

She crosses her arms over her chest. "Sunday," she acknowledges me. "I need to get going soon, before anyone starts questioning my absence."

"Thank you." Darius stands and offers her a quick hug. "We know this could have gotten you into deep shit, but we appreciate it."

"I won't let those fuckers kill anybody else if I can help it, but there's not much more I can do. This is bigger than any of us." Veronica offers me a wary smile. "Be careful, okay? I don't know what they plan on doing next."

She grabs her bag I hadn't seen before off the ground and leaves, shutting the door behind her.

I shift anxiously, forgetting that I am in Axel's lap.

"Cut it out." He bites the words out and his sturdy hands find my waist holding me in place.

"I think it's time you both told me what's going on."

Darius retakes his place next to us. "We need to," he speaks the words to Axel.

"No, we fucking don't."

"Julia isn't on vacation." Those aren't the words I expect Darius to say.

Axel's hold on my waist tightens, his fingertips digging into my skin. I can feel their heat through the thin material of my shirt.

"What do you mean?" It feels as if bugs are scattering across my skin.

"She's gone." Axel's words are cruel. "And it is best you accept that."

"She's not gone. She's on vacation with her parents." My tone turns harsh. Julia is the last tether I have to my life before Auggie and Tripp's deaths.

"No, her parents are on that vacation. All expenses paid by their employers, the Thornes." Axel's voice thunders against my back.

I no longer want to be in his lap. Darius, who has been watching the entire interaction, attempts to tear me from Axel's arms.

Axel growls, "Fuck off."

"Give her to me, she needs to feel safe and you're not good at that." The words have their desired affect and Axel's hold loosens enough for Darius to pull me into his embrace.

He cradles me against him, the way he holds me is reminiscent of how one might hold a baby.

I guess that's what I am, a blubbering baby. "What happened?" The words are barely audible.

Darius squeezes me comfortingly. He checks over his shoulder to ensure the door is shut before he begins.

The ventilator's steady beeping in the background has ramped up the chaos swirling in my brain. What does he mean Julia is gone? That doesn't make any sense.

"I'm guessing you saw the pictures of the girls and the men holding the drinks?" The question is rhetoric. Before I can ask how he knows he continues, "Auggie and Tripp showed us. We all long since knew that this town is a cesspool of evil, but we had never guessed at its depths."

"So girls are just getting assaulted left and right? It's fucking horrible, but what makes that any different than any other place in the fucking world?"

"Because that's not all it is, you stupid girl!" Axel leans forward, his scorching breath fanning my lips. "That's just the first step. Creating victims. If you have been victimized once. It's easier for it to happen again and again!"

If it weren't for Darius's hold on me, I would have fallen to the ground.

My mouth opens and closes a few times. I'm not sure what to say. "What *exactly* does that mean?"

The ventilator whooshes and beeps.

It reminds me of an accordion.

"Axel." Darius's rough fingers begin to stroke my skin. His tone is warning.

"Oh, now this is too much? Well, what were you going to fucking tell her? That bad men do bad things? Well, news flash, that *never* works. She's a grown ass adult."

"She's a teenager!" Darius yells. I flinch away from his anger, but his strong grip holds me in place.

"We're all teenagers! Tripp and Auggie were teenagers! All the girls they kidnap are teenagers!"

"Stop yelling," I whisper out hoarsely. I can't handle it. It's too much.

Axel's bright eyes flicker to mine. They are a prism of indeterminate pain.

"Wildflower, they're targeting victims. They have the younger generation do their dirty work. Assault the girls, set them up for desperation, depression. And then—" Darius stutters.

"And then when they're at their lowest? They lure the girls into an offer they can't refuse, but that offer? It's the last step. The last step until they're sold."

I choke on my own spit, I cough a few times. Sold? That happened to Julia? To countless others we know? "But that's not possible. We would notice girls going missing. There would be an uproar, they couldn't keep it hidden."

"Oh, really? And how many stories have you heard of people here leaving town and cutting all ties? About all of these wonderful scholarships to places far, far away?" Axel's voice is sharp.

"I...I..." I think about it, about Tiffany. A lot of people from high school did go off to college, and most of them never came back. I always thought they hated this town like I did, but what if it was something more? "Still. Someone had to have noticed."

"They do." Darius presses his lips to my earlobe, he snuggles against it for a moment. "Then they go missing too. Or they end up in jail."

Axel laughs humorlessly.

"Or they die—" Darius pauses "—in *accidents*."

The accordion of the ventilator echoes around the room. An eerie tune. Another beep. Grayson's chest rising and falling.

"Are they going to kill us?" I mutter the words turning into Darius's chest, burying myself in his shirt, breathing him in. He still has me cradled in his arms. It's the only thing holding me together at all. Keeping me from a meltdown.

"No," Axel barks the word. "But you can't be stupid anymore. You can't walk right into their traps."

"Why do I feel like there's more?" I pull my face from Darius's shirt and watch him carefully.

He leans down pressing his forehead to mine. "There is, but can you please trust us when we say we're just trying to keep you safe?"

I hate that fucking word. Safe. But I don't want to argue anymore. Not here. Not now.

"Okay, but isn't there something we can do? Where are they taken? What about Julia? I need to get her back, to save her."

"There is. There are still good people in this town. Parents are growing suspicious. Why are all the kids in this town suddenly cutting ties and leaving when they graduate? They think it's a cult." Darius's voice is careful, he closes his eyes, breathing in and out slowly. I inexplicably know he isn't telling me everything, but he's right.

I need to trust them.

"What do we do now?" I finally untangle myself from Darius's hold. He helps me to my feet, and I lean over Grayson.

Laying in the bed like this he looks so vulnerable. His presence always takes up so much more space than his body, and right now, he looks too small. It is incredibly jarring.

I place a chaste kiss on his forehead. I turn back around.

"We lay low. We work at the marina. We go about our day-to-day lives. We wait for Grayson to wake up." Axel stands up and jerks forward, grabbing my hand. He places a soft delicate kiss on the back of it before rubbing it against his face. "There's one more thing you need to know."

"Don't," Darius orders.

This time Axel listens and lowers my hand. Electricity tingles in his wake. "You heard Dare-Bear. Guess I'll have to keep a few things close to the chest." The words are sarcastic. *Mocking*.

"Come on, let's go." Darius stands to his full height, stretching.

"We can't leave him here alone," I argue.

"I'll be staying with him, Little Lamb. He'll be awake and out of here soon enough. Keep the marina's kitchen running for me would you?" Axel asks before swooping forward, capturing my lips with his.

I barely react. His mouth is hot, sharp, strong. He reaches up, tangling in my curls, his other hand going to the back of my neck. He devours me.

His tongue is a flame as it pushes into my mouth assaulting me with a vengeance. I can't tell if it is passion or concern that pushes the kiss deeper.

It swirls through my nerves, my core clenches around nothing, I moan into his mouth.

He groans back, squeezing my neck tightly, tugging us even closer together.

"Axel." Darius's voice is annoyed. Exasperated.

I try to pull back, but Axel holds me in place. He offers one more peck and then bites down on my bottom lip.

"Mmm. I'm going to miss you while I'm here." He lets me go and Darius is there to steady me. My knees are weak and if it weren't for Darius's hold, I would fall to the ground. "Take care of her," he directs over my shoulder.

"Always," Darius promises. "We'll see you soon."

"Yeah in two wee—"

I can't hear the rest of what Axel says because Darius wrenches me out the door.

I hear Axel let out a loud enraged growl before the door slinks shut behind us.

My lips are still tingling from his kiss.

My guilt is ever present, forming a knot in my stomach. My heart is weighed down with the horror that makes up this town. My mind is swirling with concern for Julia, for all the girls.

But most of all? I am angry. Enraged.

How dare the Thornes hurt my brother? How dare the sheriff help them?

I will be listening to the O'Briens. I will not put them in harm's way, but the second I see a way that I can? I will be exacting my revenge.

Because if justice can't be served, I will have to create my own.

Part III Acceptance

July 19th

I t's been two weeks.

I have spent the time with Darius, growing closer and closer by the moment. His face is finally almost back to its normal color, and he can walk steadily again.

He hasn't kissed me or *touched* me since the day after that horrible river party, but I can tell he's holding back.

He's respecting my boundaries.

I almost wish he wouldn't.

"Runners!" I jump at the sound of Darius's voice. I'm working in the restaurant at their marina, covered in sweat, but it is so freeing. An adrenaline rush as the patrons keep flooding in and the orders never stop flowing.

A distraction from the fact Grayson hasn't woken up yet.

"Sunday." I don't look up from my plating as Darius steps up next to me. He begins loading up a different tray. Our elbows brush in the small space; the contact is electrifying.

I do my best not to react.

I have learned a lot about the youngest O'Brien brother. He is kind, sweet, selfless.

He gave up his dreams to keep their family afloat. He is the steady voice that pulls Grayson and Axel out of altercations. He is someone I can rely on.

I am no longer angry at any of the brothers for hiding the truth of this town from me, I recognize it was for my own good. Instead, I have redirected my fury.

The dinner rush takes me back into the lull of mindless motion. Loading trays. Garnishing plates. Calling for food runners.

Darius comes and goes as the night progresses, and all too soon, the tickets crawl to a stop.

"You good munchkin?" Rick, one of the cooks, asks sweetly across the line. He was here on my first day too. The older man looks like Santa Claus, but he is an asshole to everyone. Except me.

"Oh, knock it off, Axel will throw a hissy if you're too sweet on her." Wayne is the other cook I met with Axel my first day at this marina. Both of the men are harmless, and they've helped me tremendously in Axel and Grayson's absence. They have been doing their best to cheer me up and keep me busy when I'm here.

I flash them a toothy smile. "He's not here to say anything." I laugh.

"Oh, is that right?"

I spin away from the cooks and my eyes meet Axel's intense ones, before climbing past him to a bulky admonishing man.

"Grayson." A hole in my heart I didn't even realize existed begins to fill at the sight of him. He still has a few bandages, and he's discolored all over, but he's here. His eyes are open. He's on his own two feet.

Without much thought, I rip off my apron and take a running start before launching at him.

He flinches, but catches me.

"Oh, I'm so sorry!" Suddenly embarrassed I try to pull away, but his arms wrap tightly around me and he lifts me until I am forced to wrap my legs around him.

"Grayson." Axel's voice is dark and laden with emotion.

Grayson pays him no mind. He uses one hand to secure me, cupping my ass in the process. The other he uses to wipe my sweaty hair from my face and tuck my curls behind both ears. One at a time.

"I missed you, baby girl. I'm so glad to see that you're okay."

I look deep into Grayson's eyes. I can see the depth of his exhaustion. His worry.

"Of course, I am. Why wouldn't I be?"

He presses his forehead to mine. "You can be so stubborn. I was afraid you might do something *unwise*."

"You mean stupid," Axel cuts in. He moves until he is at my back, sandwiching me between the two brothers. I don't argue because I can tell Axel is helping hold my weight up. Grayson isn't fully healed. But he's awake. Grayson is awake.

"Well, either you three can clean the kitchen for us or can you get out of our way," Rick gripes behind me.

"Sorry Rick!" I try to twist my head, but I can't see past the brute that is Axel.

"Not your fault, munchkin."

Axel stiffens at my back. "What did you just call her?"

I reach behind me and try to untangle myself from the men, but they don't let me. "Put me down, please? I need a shower and to change."

Axel stuffs his head into my neck, licking a line up the side. "No, I think you're perfect just like this."

This close, Grayson can't hide his emotions as well as he usually does or maybe it's because he still isn't fully recovered. Either way the yearning in his eyes is unmistakable. And even more so, his cock that is slowly hardening.

I roll once against it.

Grayson growls, but it has the desired effect and he jumps back. I have just enough time to get my feet underneath me as I fall against Axel.

The guilt is still a pit in my stomach. I shouldn't be putting myself in these situations with the brothers. But I can't help it.

They are the last of what I have. My only tether to this world. They are the reason I am any semblance of okay.

Grayson's strength. It offers me the ability to stand on my own two feet.

Axel's forcefulness. It makes me realize that it's okay to live in each moment.

Darius's calm. It gives me a safe place to always return to.

"Come on Wildflower, let me take you home." Darius steps into the small space, filling it up the rest of the way with his presence.

Axel tries to hold onto me, but Darius tugs me free. "You two, shut it down. I'll get her home safe."

I offer one more backwards look to both brothers.

Grayson mindlessly reaches out and traces a path down my arm before Darius is tugging me away.

I am happier than I have been in weeks; I missed Grayson and Axel more than I realized.

My heart and brain are churning masses of confusion and doubt.

I can't love more than one man, can I?

As soon as the thought lands in my mind, I throw it as far away as possible. It isn't right.

What the fuck is wrong with me?

July 19th

"Have you opened your gift from your brother yet?" Darius's question catches me off guard.

"No." I expel the word as I step inside the house. I shut the door quickly behind us. A creepy feeling has taken hold since we left the restaurant. I can't shake that something bad is going to happen.

It makes no sense. Grayson woke up. Everything is right in the world. The three brothers are all back under one roof. It wasn't only Grayson I hadn't seen for two weeks, it was Axel too. He kept his word, never leaving his brother's side.

"I think you should." Darius leads us to my room, he doesn't stop once inside and makes his way to the box that is in a corner of the room, the letter is inside. He leans down and hands it to me.

I look down at the envelope and up at Darius. I blink a few times.

Once I open this, there will be nothing left. It was hard enough with Tripp, to know that reading his letter was the last time I would ever have anything new from him. His life ended at the last word written out on that paper.

How will it feel without Auggie? We spent eighteen years together. He was the best brother I could ever have asked for. He didn't deserve any of this to happen. He was just trying to fix a broken world. He was just a kid.

A teardrop falls onto the envelope. I use the back of my arm to wipe my face. I look up to see Darius now sitting on my bed, his arms open for me.

I don't think. I dive into the comfort he offers. He cradles me, sweeping lines in comforting strokes up and down my back.

"I'm sorry, I thought you would be ready," he murmurs the words into my hair as he peppers kisses there. He moves his lips until he places a chaste kiss onto my cheek.

"That's the thing, I think I am. How am I already ready? He's been gone less than two months. Why does it feel like it's been years?"

Darius stills underneath me. Something I said has caught him off guard, but then he continues the path of kisses.

"I'm sweaty and gross and I should really not be on your lap."

"You're fine, I smell nothing." He buries his nose into my ear and inhales. It tickles and I attempt to wriggle away.

"Oh, hold still." He wraps his arms around me keeping me in place.

One hand still holds the envelope, but I free the other to trace a corded muscular arm. "You don't have any tattoos?"

"I have two," Darius advises.

I twist until I can look him in the eyes. "Where? I haven't seen any."

Uncertainty washes across his face before he lets out an exasperated sigh. "I know you won't let it go."

He separates us enough so that he can lift up his shirt a bit. Before I am too distracted by his toned abdomen, my attention is stolen by his tattoos.

Over his heart is an array of blue wildflowers. Above it is the month and day of Tripp and Axel's birthday.

My fingers go up to trace it.

A noise escapes his lips as if he were going to moan but bit it back at the last moment.

I haven't seen a lot of tattoos, besides the O'Briens', but I can tell it's fresh.

"When did you get this?" I whisper.

"The morning of the memorial."

Confusion sweeps through me. Wildflowers. Is it because of the tattoo he calls me that? He certainly didn't know me the day of the memorial. It was the first time I had a real conversation with any of the brothers, minus Tripp.

He reaches out, grabbing my hand, pulling it from his skin, before yanking his shirt back down. "You ready?"

The envelope is slightly crushed now and I frown at the sight. But I find that I am ready.

I am calm.

I open it.

July 19th

Something falls to the floor, but I focus my attention on the letter.

Hey lil sis,

Life is a weird fucking thing. Am I right? The weirdest part is that this is both a present and a possible goodbye.

I need to go away for a while. I want you to come with me, but I don't know if that will be safe either.

Whatever happens, I want you to know that I fucking love the shit out of you. And if something ever goes down, I need you to trust the O'Briens. All of them. Oh and I know about you and Tripp. You aren't that sly, I got a present that hopefully the two of you will enjoy. Fuck, Sunflower, one of my best friends? The rest of them better keep their promise and keep their grimy fuckwad hands off you or I will be kicking all their asses.

Okay less threatening murder. Here's time for a serious talk. You need to be careful. Our town isn't safe. There is some disgusting shit going on. If it ever gets too bad, I need you to go to the O'Briens', they may be dumb shits but I trust them all. They will keep you safe.

Fuck. Sorry this sucked, but uh. Happy graduation!

Love you!
-Auggie

I fold the letter carefully, setting it on the bed before reaching down and grabbing what fell.

Two tickets to the space center and planetarium.

They fall back to the floor and I pay no mind to Darius as I stumble to the bathroom.

He's there to pull my hair back as I puke into the toilet. He keeps hold of my hair as he reaches over and turns the shower on.

I dry heave a few more times before I finally get myself under control.

"My stupid. Ignorant. White knight. Brother." I throw the words into the porcelain below. I wipe my mouth and flush the toilet.

I need a shower.

I don't want to be alone.

"Will you stay?"

Darius looks unsure for a moment before offering a curt nod.

He pushes himself up and onto the counter crossing his legs. His heels swinging back and forth and tapping against the wooden drawers below. The noise is oddly cathartic.

"Eyes shut please." I trust him to not peek, but even if he does, he's seen me half naked before. I turn away from him and strip, stepping into the steaming shower, and shutting the curtain. I can't see him through it, just his outline.

Tap. Tap. Tap.

The rhythm of his feet against the drawers continues.

"He knew he was going to die," I state into the shower head.

"He suspected." Darius voice is calm, soothing.

"Why didn't you stop him?" It's not a fair question.

"Just like we can stop you?" Darius laughs humorlessly. "Besides that, Tripp was just as bad."

"When did this all start?" The water is turning my skin red, but I pay it no mind. I need to cleanse.

"When Axel went to jail. Mark, he—" Darius pauses, I can tell he doesn't want to continue, even the tapping of his feet stops.

I finish washing my hair, I watch the soap as it goes down the drain.

"I need to know."

"Carrie. She was raped. By Mark. Carrie didn't even remember any of it happening. Auggie let her believe it was them hooking up, but it ruined their relationship."

I should have expected it, but I don't. The words shock me so fully that I somehow lose my footing, but before I can fall backwards, Darius is jumping forward and catching us.

The sound of us, tumbling echoes around the bathroom.

It isn't long before I hear stomping outside, in my bedroom. Before I can even gather myself to scream to stop, Axel is marching his way into the room.

"You clumsy fucking girl. Stop falling in bathtubs." This time the déjà vu makes sense when he yanks me up and off of Darius.

"I'm good," Darius groans softly. "Not that you asked." He's wrapped in the shower curtain half soaked and sprawled on the tub.

"I don't fucking care. You were supposed to wait." Axel begins examining me, his hands on my shoulders as he checks me up and down and I take this moment to remember that I am stark naked.

"Fuck, you're too fucking beautiful for your own good. You look like an innocent angel, but you're not, are you?" Axel's eyes darken and his fingers on my shoulders begin to stroke circles across my skin. "I heard what Darius made you do, and I'm jealous. I can't wait to make you cum all over my fingers. My face. My *cock*." Other than my cheeks heating, I don't have time to react; he drags me forward, pressing me into him.

My nipples meet leather. My thighs, scratchy jeans. I don't realize I'm panting, until I hear him chuckling in my ear.

"You like that, don't you?"

"Axel," Darius warns. I hear him getting up behind us, but I am captivated in Axel's attention.

"Hmmm, I just want a little taste."

I gulp, but don't move.

"She's not ready. She just read the letter."

The words are a bucket of iced root beer. Sticky, distracting, uncomfortable.

Axel grumbles but lets me go. He reaches behind me and grabs a towel. I allow him to secure it in place.

"Come on, you need to get dressed. Grayson won't like this." Axel pushes me out of the bathroom.

"No, he certainly won't." Grayson leans against the door frame of my bedroom, he takes up the entirety of it.

Before, he was in shorts and a T-shirt, but now in a long sleeve and sweats. I can no longer make out any visible injuries. But I know that they're there. Maybe I didn't make them, but I was the cause.

"Grayson, I'm sorry." I am incredibly full of useless apologies.

"Put some clothes on Sunday." The anger in his voice is palpable and I suddenly find it exceptionally difficult to swallow.

I separate from Axel and make it to the closet, changing quickly.

I can hear bits and pieces about the letter, but they're whispering and go quiet as soon as I step back out.

Suddenly, again, everything is too much. I feel suffocated by the three men staring at me.

Do they even want me here?

Or was it the last stupid wish of my idiotic brother.

I move past Axel and go to the window in a trance. I don't even realize I'm sliding it up and pulling myself onto the roof until I feel the pressure of hands on my hips, helping to push me to the flat part of the roof. I almost stumble, but the security of his hands keeps me safe.

"Easy, you're too clumsy for this shit."

Why Axel is the one they sent after me, I don't understand.

"Grayson tried to strong arm me up here, but the ass is in more pain than he lets on."

The shingles aren't exactly comfortable as I ease my way into a sitting position, but I don't care.

Axel shoulders out of his leather jacket and lays it on the roof behind us. "Come here."

He doesn't wait for me, yanking me down and against his side.

"I miss them."

Axel breathes in and out a few times and I turn to watch him. "I know. It's so hard to remember that it's not their fault, but I can't help but to be angry. To blame them for all of this." I can tell his words hold a deeper meaning. Like he isn't talking about their deaths but something else entirely that I am not privy to. It's in the way he watches me with his intense vibrant eyes, in the cruel curl of his lips, in his ruthless tone.

I know better than to question him. I look away, focusing my attention on the sky above.

The stars are especially bright and distracting. I don't react to his words. To what he is saying or what he is hiding from me. Instead, I lift a hand and trace different constellations with my finger. Allowing myself a moment of peace. I start with the Gemini constellation, my birth sign, then once I have it sketched, I move to the Leo.

"The lion," I murmur.

Axel chuckles softly. "That's the only one I used to know, but I've learned a lot." The words yet again seem to hold a deeper meaning, but I continue the Leo's path.

Once complete, I twist to Axel. "You, Tripp, and my brother are all Leos. Lions."

"You know what happens to a lion in a cage?" Axel shoots back at me, rolling on his side to fully face me. The air between us is charged. Static. Electric. His hand moves gently to my cheek. He presses his lips to mine in a hot searing kiss before pulling away. "They break."

"You're not broken," I bite the words at him. *He's not.*

Axel rolls onto his back, ending the moment. "Aren't I?" He snorts caustically and the next thing I know he is reaching over and yanking me onto him.

I am so used to being manhandled by these men I don't make any noise as I find my balance. My hands and knees are no longer protected by the leather jacket and they dig into the sharp shingles as I hover over Axel. My eyes go to his. He's not crying, but the glassiness is evidence of his pain.

His strong hands come up, one caresses the bottom of my ass in slow strokes, the other finds my neck, pulling us closer together. "Only a broken monster would covet such a beautiful creature. You know I haven't said it to you in so many words, but I love you, Little Lamb. I will for however many lifetimes I can."

His words are a slap to the face. "I—I—" I stutter out. I don't know what to say. "We still barely know each other."

Axel hums in annoyance. "You know more about me than any other living person. That includes my brothers. The only one that knew me better was Tripp. But here's the thing, I have watched you for years. But you never lifted your eyes. You never met my gaze. Did you know I was destined to be broken? Did you know there was no saving my soul? Is that why you fell for Tripp?" He tugs me even closer until our noses are touching and I'm forced to close my eyes.

"I didn't know," I whisper out hoarsely. "I thought you all hated me. That's why you were never inviting me around."

"Augustus made us promise. *'Don't date my sister you fuckwads, not one of you is good enough for her.'* Well, he was partially right, maybe not one of us, but what about us all?"

"What do you mean?" I gulp, trying to escape from him.

The hand on my ass moves a little lower, but it keeps me in place. Desire courses through me.

I shouldn't want Axel.

I shouldn't want Darius.

I shouldn't want Grayson.

This is all so incredibly wrong. I was with their brother. With Axel's twin.

Axel laughs out loud. A sharp bellowing noise that vibrates through me in a delicious fashion. His cock is slowly hardening as we continue this conversation. It pokes me in the belly, and once more, I try to escape his hold.

"No, Sunday. You're done running away. Open your fucking eyes."

They flash open. His typical bright ones are engulfed in darkness. The stars and moon are our only source of light.

"I want to fuck you." The words rush into the air. "Right here, right now. I want to watch you take my dick like I know you can. I want to consume your screams as I push you too far and fill you past the point of comfort. I need it, more than I need this fucking air, or this fucking life. But I am waiting for you to figure out that this is exactly what you want." Axel is glowering at me.

We are still so incredibly close that each inhale I am swallowing more of his words. I am acutely aware of the pain in my palms and knees from the roof, but I pay it no mind. His declaration has caused neediness to be the predominant feeling coursing through my body.

I come to a stark and shocking realization.

I *want* him to fuck me.

His lips curl into a knowing cruel smile. "But it's not just me. It's Darius and Grayson, too. They both want you. Whether they will admit it to you or not. So Augustus was right–each of us, we could never deserve a woman like you, but the three of us together? I want you to think on it."

He rolls his hips upwards, the friction is exactly where I need it and I let out a raspy moan.

"Soon, when you're ready, I want a repeat of this, but I want my dick to be buried so deep inside of you that it hurts. Because, my Little Lamb, I am going to be the most vicious of us, but I promise you will love every minute of it."

His hand on my ass has made its way to the apex of my thighs. He moves his long fingers until they curl around my cunt, cupping it.

"I can't wait to own this."

I need more.

I try to push into his hand, but he pulls it away and I let out an embarrassing whimper.

"Nuh uh uh, not until you're ready to accept us all. Now, it's time to rejoin my brothers."

I want to argue, to scream and yell, but he's right. I'm not ready for him, for any of this. I'm not convinced Grayson really wants anything to do with me. I'm still a guilty mess filled with anger and grief and sadness.

We carefully make our way back inside the room through the window. I'm not surprised to see that both brothers are still there.

Darius takes me into his arms providing the calming relief I need, he gives both of my cheeks a soft kiss. "Be good, please."

He lets me go, but now I am in Axel's tight hold, being squeezed just to the point of pain. "Think about it." He grabs my ass and pulls me flush to him, pushing his hot lips to mine for just an instant.

"What the fuck?" Grayson's voice cuts into the moment.

Axel's smile is all teeth before he takes Darius by the forearm and drags him out of the room. "You two need to *talk*. She doesn't think you *like* her."

My cheeks flush. "I didn't say that."

"Oh, shut the fuck up it was plain as day on your face as I talked about fucking you. About all of us fucking you." Axel doesn't stop, he's out the door with Darius and slamming it behind them before Grayson can let loose his anger.

"Tell me he didn't." Grayson turns on me.

A moment ago he was leaning against my closet door, but now he is stepping into my space. I move backwards until the back of my legs hits the bed. "I know that I am nothing but a nuisance to you. A financial and emotional burden. That I almost got you killed. That it's my fault Darius was hurt. That I'm the reason Auggie and Tripp were killed. That they wouldn't have been here if it weren't for me."

Grayson grouses, "No." He's towering over me now, his large rough hands come up grabbing my arms. "Next you're going to blame yourself for hurricanes and car accidents and murders. None of that is your fault. There are certain strands of fate that are inevitable, whether you tugged on them or not, I would have gotten my ass beat by Maxwell and Mark. The only difference is that you weren't with me when it happened. You were safe. You *are* safe." His voice is coated in emotion. "And don't you dare call yourself a nuisance. You are the brightest part of our lives. Kind, compassionate, *stubborn*."

I'm not sure if he realizes he's shaking me.

An unhinged laugh escapes my throat. "The brightest part? I'm an angry, grief-riddled, guilty idiot. I can't do anything right! Even though we had been growing distant, my best friend has apparently been missing for months, and I didn't even know." My voice pitches, getting louder as the words leave my lips. "You all have been in my orbit for years and I never even looked your way. Never saw the pain you all must be going through."

I stare at Grayson. He is the eldest brother. He is the one that keeps them protected as best he can. Who looks out for him?

"What about you, Grayson? What do you want? Because half the time I didn't think you wanted me around, but then you slept every night in this room with me. Then you risked yourself for me. Then you were always there showing up when I needed you most." I'm no longer furious, but my voice is loud, coated in emotion. "So, tell me Grayson, if nothing else outside this room existed, what would you want?" I scream the words into his face, I may not be angry, but I am annoyed. Irritated. My cheeks heated in frustration.

His grip on my arms tightens. A circus of emotion tumbles in my stomach.

He drops his hold and turns around.

Pain. Rejection. Disappointment. They pound their way through the walls around my heart. The walls I erected the day Tripp and Auggie died.

"You," he speaks the word at the window.

"What?" I snap out. I'm tired of whatever this is. I'm exhausted.

He spins back around ignoring his injuries, launching himself forward. He pushes me back on the mattress. His lips press against mine.

Confusion bubbles up, but the feel of his hands pushing under the fabric of my shirt distracts me.

His mouth is searing as he deepens the kiss. His calloused fingers trace patterns up and down my skin. Axel already wound me up, but this? This is excruciating. I need more. I can't take this anymore.

"Grayson," I pant the word against his lips as he pulls back slowly. I reach up to tangle my hands into his soft hair. He nuzzles his face against mine, the scratchiness of his beard leaving a trail of tingling pleasure.

"I want you, baby girl. But you're too young. I'm twenty-six years old, a grown man that needs to be watching over you. Taking care of you. I shouldn't be doing *this*." One hand has made its way inside my bra, his actions at odds with his words, he kneads the nipple, pinching it lightly. "But I can't help myself anymore. You are so vibrant and full of energy. You are the only good that is in my life. I am drawn to you. The first thing I wanted when I woke up was to find you and tell you how I feel. But that isn't right. *This* isn't right."

The rejection is acid along my skin. I let my eyelids fall until I can barely make out his form. I don't want to hear anymore.

"You aren't understanding." Grayson pushes his lips to mine again, this time he is slow, carefully moving mine against his. The hand in my bra pinches down, hard. I gasp into his mouth. His other hand moves to my hair. He grabs hold of it tenderly. He ends the kiss. I watch as he brings a single curl to his lips, kissing it. "You deserve better than us. But unfortunately for you? We're never going to let you leave. I know I shouldn't want you, baby girl, but that doesn't change the fact that I do."

He kisses me gently on the nose before carefully getting up off of me.

I am in shock. My lips are tingling. My core is throbbing in neediness.

My brain is in emotional turmoil. I don't know how or what I'm supposed to feel, but then my eyes find his pants. Find that his cock has hardened to an impressive length.

It instills confidence as I sit up and reach forward, grabbing hold of Grayson.

There's guilt still thumping its way into my heart, but I accept it. Accept that what I am doing is wrong.

I tug Grayson closer and he lets me. He seems confused by what I'm doing, until I reach my other hand up.

With me sitting on the bed and him standing, his cock is staring me in the face through his pants.

"Sunday," he expels the word. It's a warning.

I don't listen.

Carefully I pull his pants down. They're all that he's wearing, and his hardened cock bobs out.

It's impressive and I begin to second guess what I'm doing, but then I look up and find Grayson watching me. His eyes hooded and coated in lust.

It is heady. To have such a profound man want me.

Carefully, ever so slowly, I open my mouth and guide the tip of his cock in.

"Sunday," he groans my name in appreciation.

I move my head down as far as I can go until the tip is lodged in the very back of my throat, and I do my best to swallow around it. I've never actually done this before, but Grayson's groans of appreciation are guiding my way.

"Suck it down, use your tongue," Grayson growls out.

Following his instructions, I hollow my cheeks and suck, swirling my tongue and bringing my other hand up to cover the area my mouth can't reach.

"Fuck!" Before he let me keep my own pace, but I have set him off. "Fucking tap me if you need me to stop." That's the only warning I get before he grabs the back of my head and wraps his large hands in my hair. I do my best to open my mouth as he proceeds to fuck my throat with ruthless abandon.

My eyes are watering, spit is dribbling down my chin, but above all else, my desire is surging.

Making Grayson lose his cool, having him so engrossed in this moment, giving pleasure to such a solitary man, it isn't enough to make me sporadically come, but it is making me crave more than this.

Grayson grunts when I am just at the point of tapping out. "Take all of this. You better not waste any."

I don't have any time to question his words as his cock pulses in my mouth and warm liquid fills the back of my throat. I do my best to swallow around him, but I gag a bit before he pulls free. A string of his cum falls from my lips. Grayson leans down and wipes it up, pushing it back into my mouth.

"Swallow." The word is a command that I follow.

His finger lingers in my mouth another moment before he slowly removes it. "You're going to ruin me."

I don't understand what he means. I am still processing what has just happened. I am trying to contain the throbbing that is pushing me to go further with Grayson, but I realize I'm not quite ready for that.

The guilt has returned.

Grayson tugs his pants back up and offers me a knowing smile.

"Come here, let's just sit and watch a show. We go at your pace, but yes Sunday, I care about you, more than you know. And I want you, more of you, all of you. Whenever you are ready, but there's no rush." He helps me to readjust into a more comfortable position on the bed, he puts on a movie before joining me.

I still have not processed what just happened so instead, I pivot to what has been on my mind from before. "I opened my gift."

Grayson looks down at me, his eyebrows furrowed together in concern. "I know," he states warily.

"I would like to go with you, when you're feeling better that is. To the space center."

"You would?" For the second time since I have met Grayson, I seemed to have truly shocked him. His voice is pitched and uneven. "You're not going to just run off alone?"

"No?" I ask, confused. While I had thought of that before I went onto the roof, the last few hours changed my mind. "You don't have to if you don't want to, but I thought it could be nice. We could make it a fun day?" My voice is suddenly unsure.

Grayson squeezes me to him. "I would love to go, baby girl. I just didn't expect you to ask me."

"I want to wait a few weeks though." I want to wait until he is fully healed, but I don't add that part out loud.

"Of course." He kisses my forehead, before we both return our attention to the screen. Under the blanket his leg presses against mine, his arms wrap around me, and I fall comfortably into the security and safety that is Grayson.

August 13th

The pavement is cold, scratchy, painful.

I try to move my limbs. I can't. I can't feel anything.

I'm lying face up, staring at the stars. I use my eyes to search my surroundings, the only thing that I can move. About ten feet away in my periphery, I see a black shape. It appears to be a person, but I can't tell in the darkness, and I can't really look at it.

There is one lone street light. It flickers above me. I try to rasp in air, nothing happens.

My attention drifts downwards, I can see the color red, but I can't make out where it's coming from.

"Here she is. Help me with her." The voice is comforting, warm.

I can't feel anything when I'm lifted up, at least not physically, but something in my chest heats. An emotion unravels.

"I've got her." Tripp's soothing voice floats to me. "Oh, Sunflower, please stop meeting us here."

"Lil sis, you read the letter? I'm sorry about the dramatics, I was afraid that I would go missing too. I didn't expect this." Auggie squats before me, he's wearing his hoodie from college, he ruffles my hair. "It seems you're doing okay, I have a good feeling, but you need to listen to me."

Tripp leans me a bit more forward, my eyes catch on the crimson. The blood seeping out of my white shirt. I want to scream, but I can't say anything, I can't move.

"It's okay, you're okay." Tripp's palliating voice in my ear is the only thing that keeps my mind from crumbling.

"Sis, Sunflower, you need to listen to me. You need to be careful. The next twenty-four hours are going to come at you fast. Whatever you do, keep your head down. Don't follow any leads. Don't go anywhere without telling the O'Briens. If you get an idea, you need to call Grayson. Do you understand me?" Auggie is shouting the words at me. It's the most aggressive he's ever been.

I don't understand anything.

"Lighten up, she's not going to remember this anyways." Tripp's voice is still mollifying, it settles my nerves. "It's going to be okay Sunflower, no matter what happens we will be here for you."

Remorse presses against my chest, my vision blurs. It isn't from tears.

"Hush, I can feel you. Feel your pain, your guilt. There's nothing to be ashamed of, they always owned pieces of your heart, you just didn't know it. Who do you think always kept the bullies away? The evil of this town? Well, it was Auggie sure, but it was also me, Axel, Darius, Grayson." I hear as Tripp whooshes air out of his chest behind me. "You need each other. Now that we're gone, rely on each other. I would tell you to leave this town and never look back, but even if you remember this, I know none of you will listen. Too damn stubborn." Tripp chuckles.

Auggie offers a wistful smile. "It's going to be okay, Sunflower. Just keep your head down, and please, whatever you do, don't go off alone." He leans forward hugging me.

I can't feel anything and the scene fades into blackness.

I try to look at my surroundings as my vision disappears.

A flickering light. A bend. One side is a forest, the other side is an embankment. The guard rail is bent. A body lies in a puddle on the ground. I recognize them.

My heart drops into my stomach.

I wake up screaming.

"Come here, it's okay."

Grayson's familiar scent fills my nostrils, his body is pressed against my front. I wrap my arms around him as I tremble.

"Shhhh, it's okay. It's okay. Do you want to talk to me about it?" He speaks the words softly into my ear as I burrow my face into his chest.

His injuries have finally healed.

I haven't done anything more with the brothers since Grayson came home from the hospital, but I feel closer to them all, nonetheless. We have kept it platonic. The ball is essentially in my court—except with Grayson—but I'm not ready.

"Nightmare?" he asks into my hair.

"Yeah." The word is shaky, but gradually I am calming down.

"You've been getting them more and more, are you sure we should go today?" Grayson isn't wrong, almost every morning I wake up in distress.

Today feels especially unpleasant.

"You still can't remember anything from them?"

How do I explain the feelings that follow me. The terror, uneasiness, the dread. It wouldn't make any sense, I would sound crazy.

"Work?" I ask, finally extracting myself from Grayson's safety now that my nerves have calmed. A bit.

"Not today, you have been going nonstop. Today we both are going to play hooky." Grayson sits up, heaving me into his lap and wrapping his arms around me.

Platonic.

He nuzzles his face into my neck. His breath skirting down the column of my neck.

Friendly.

His cock hardens against my ass as his grip on me tightens.

I try to roll against it, gain some type of relief. My desire is quickly outweighing the anxiety I woke up with.

He pushes me out of his lap, I startle enough to fall, but he catches me. I'm past the point of embarrassment. This is now a common ritual. Stringing me along.

He doesn't say anything as I go to the closet and get dressed.

Today is the day we are going to go to the space center.

I push the desire to jump back on Grayson down. I feel guilty enough bringing him with me today. I don't want to add anything to it. Changed and back in the room, my focus catches on the box of Auggie and Tripp's things. I walk towards it mindlessly and pull out a hoodie.

"Auggie loved that thing, he was so proud of his acceptance there." Grayson's voice is wistful.

Sometimes I forget how close they were, that they were all best friends. "For some reason I want to wear it, but it will be too hot, won't it?"

Grayson is dressed now and leaning against the wall, he pushes off it and walks toward me. He steps up behind me and reaches down, he takes the hoodie from me and pulls it over my head.

"Wear it. I know you haven't been there without them. We will make new memories together, but that doesn't mean you need to replace the old."

Sometimes it feels like Grayson knows my deepest fear and lays it flat on the surface in a way that it is no longer so scary.

"Thank you," I murmur.

"Breakfast!" Darius's shout echoes around and I offer Grayson a small smile before he takes my hand and leads us down the stairs.

For the first time in a while I find that I am excited. Happy for the day. I love the space center and maybe I won't be there with Auggie and Tripp, but I will carry them with me. As pieces of my heart.

August 13th

"Be safe, and don't keep her out too long." I try to figure out where the typical bad boy Axel has gone, because in his place is a worried mother. Instead, I focus on my breakfast. Darius is on my right eating silently, Axel to my left, and leaning against the sink facing us is Grayson.

"You know that I'm older than you right?" Grayson laughs and reaches over the counter lightly punching Axel's shoulder in the semblance of comradery.

"And you know that today is—"

The smile drops, he whips back, Grayson's eyes flicker to me. "Today is going to be a good *fun* day."

A thought courses through me. "Tomorrow is your twentieth birthday, Axel!"

And Tripp's. I don't voice that part.

I drop my fork and look to him.

He swallows his bite and swings a leg over the stool, facing me. "You going to give me a lap dance, Little Lamb?" He raises his eyebrows suggestively.

Darius reaches behind me and this time the punch that lands on Axel's shoulder sounds painful.

Axel grunts. "I'm the birthday boy, stop beating me." He inches forward pressing his shoulder to mine and leans down, nipping my ear. "Be *good*." He presses his lips to mine in a devastating scorch before jumping off the stool and retreating to the garage. A moment later, I hear the unmistakable sound of his motorcycle.

The brothers have been playing this game with me for the last several weeks. They have me on a length of rope and they keep pulling, pulling, pulling until I am on the cusp of giving in and then they drop it entirely to restart the process again.

I am frustrated, teetering on the edge of anger. But I realize what they're doing. They're making me decide. Giving me the choice to push things further.

Darius pecks me on the lips in a quick burning kiss. "Have a good day, Wildflower." His words are soft, calm, but his smile is fractured. Fake.

"What's going on?"

Grayson looks over my shoulder watching Darius leave before refocusing on me. He shrugs a shoulder. "Who knows?" He appears happy, but it doesn't reach his eyes.

I'm annoyed, but I don't say anything else and I finish my breakfast in silence.

The space center isn't as packed as it usually is. It's an hour outside of our town and something about being so far away has brought me peace.

We make it inside and through the ticketing area, we have a few hours before the planetarium show.

Now that we are here, the grief I expected to weigh me down has been replaced with excitement.

I take hold of Grayson's hand and begin dragging him to my favorite exhibits.

We stop in the space comic books and novel section first. "Do you see this? This was the first time space travel was put into a comic book, isn't this the coolest?" I continue my explanations as we make it through all the exhibits. This is one of my favorite places and my heart fills with warmth as Grayson listens intently to me jabbering on and on.

There is nothing better in the world than being able to gush over your interests without being made to feel bad about it.

"Did you know that even when they peed it was recycled into water?" I point to the sealed cups. "So, gross."

Grayson laughs. "I can't say that I did." He reaches down, ruffling my hair affectionately and I smile up at him.

This is the most fun I have had in months and I never want it to end.

Part of the center is outside and when we make our way out there, I take the hoodie off. For some reason the action seems to put Grayson on guard. "What's wrong?"

Again, I can see his anxiety. It's palpable. His furrowed brow forming a wrinkle, his hold on my hand tightening, his lips flattening. "Nothing." He casts a look around. It's as if he's expecting someone.

Usually I would want to know exactly what is going on, but I promised myself today I would just let loose. Enjoy myself. So, we continue, following the circuit until at the very bottom I see a sign for the restrooms.

Before he can fight me on it, I throw the hoodie at him and take off down the ramp to the restroom. I don't want him following me there, too, and I am half convinced he will.

"I'll be right back," I yell over my shoulder before making it through the door. I expect to come right into the bathroom, but instead it's another hallway. Straight ahead is the women's room, and to the right is an exit door to a different area. With the hood no longer blocking my periphery, I can see movement. I turn to look, and my breath stutters.

"Julia?" I haven't seen my best friend in months, but there she is. I know it's her, going through the door to the exit.

I chase after her.

I can hear Grayson calling my name, but I don't stop.

When I make it through the door, it clicks behind me and I am on the side of the space center property. In front of me is an eerily familiar hill and then just the woods. To my right is a storage shed, in the other direction is a pile of barrels. Past it, I see Julia getting into a car, I can't see the driver and I don't recognize the vehicle.

"Julia!" I call again. I go to chase after her, but a hand stops me.

"Sunday." Grayson is out of breath, but even still, his hold doesn't waver. "Stop."

When I look for Julia again, she's gone, along with the car. "It was Julia. Why did you stop me?" The adrenaline of the chase and seeing her has given way to anger. "What is wrong with you?"

Grayson whips back as if I have slapped him. The open carefree person he had slowly let out today is replaced with the guarded man I am used to. "It wasn't safe. Why would she be here?"

"Maybe you all were wrong, maybe she isn't gone. Maybe this has all been a mistake."

"Oh, baby girl." Grayson puts a sturdy hand on my shoulder the other he uses to brush my curls behind my ears. One side at a time. He presses a soft kiss to my forehead.

It's soothing, and I find my anger dissipating. He's right, she couldn't have been here, I must have been confused. But even as I think the words, another part of me knows that they're not true.

Grayson puts the hoodie back over me and offers me a quick hug. "Come on, let's go back inside, please? It's time for the show."

I offer up a soft reassuring smile. "You're probably right." Except in my gut, deep down I know that he's not. But even more than that? I know that, once more, an O'Brien is hiding something. Except, like I promised myself, I am not going to let it ruin today.

He seems to believe me and lets it go. We can't get back in from where we came, so we are forced to circle the building to the left, towards the parking lot, as we do so I get a better look at the bottom of the hill. Of the path down it.

"That looks like it would hurt to roll down." The words leave my lips unexpectedly. I can't pinpoint exactly where the thought even came from.

Grayson freezes, but then he chuckles softly. "Yes, I would imagine so."

It's the middle of summer and I am wearing a hoodie, but I can't stop the full body shudder that pulsates through my body as we pass the barrels.

The disgust that crawls up my throat. Long, slimy, tendrils.

I don't understand that I am bending over to puke until Grayson's sturdy hand is rubbing comforting circles on my back, his other holding my hair.

"It's okay, I've got you." His voice is soft, calming, grounding.

I continue on until there is nothing left in my stomach except bile. After I dry heave a few more times, I am finally able to pull myself together enough for Grayson to lift me up and carry me away. The déjà vu is getting worse, but I won't think about it today. That will be tomorrow's problem.

Only when I am in the security of his arms does the nausea leave me. Neither of us mention the incident for the rest of the day.

And I don't look at the barrels again.

August 13th

It's nearing midnight by the time we finally make it into town.

Right on cue, Grayson's phone rings. He answers it, and I can just make out Axel's voice but not the words he's saying.

"Yes, I know. We'll be home soon." Grayson casts a glance my way. "It might just be okay."

I don't pay any more attention to him because a car I recognize passes us and turns left ahead. It's the car from the space center and it's going in the direction of Julia's house.

"I need to use the bathroom," I blurt out, cutting off whatever Grayson was saying into the phone.

"We're almost home," Grayson declares firmly, not slowing down.

I point to a gas station. "Now." I start wiggling in my seat.

This might be my only chance to get answers for myself. A plan forms.

We pull up to the side of the gas station. I go to get out of the car, but Grayson follows me.

I watch him carefully as he pockets his keys. Before I can second guess myself, I launch myself at him. Wrapping my arms and legs around him. He catches me with a startled grunt.

"What—"

I cut him off with my lips. I try to put as much passion and emotion as I possibly can into the kiss. I want him to know that this isn't goodbye, that I care about him.

That I love him.

The thought startles me, but I don't stop.

I realize in this moment that I love all of the O'Brien brothers. I am *in* love with them all. This time, I accept the guilt that floods me, and for some reason, it doesn't affect me as much as it usually does.

Grayson carries me to the hood of his car and my ass rests on it as we explore each other. One of my hands goes to the back of his head, the other traces lines up and down his chest and abdomen before slowly moving further south.

I gently grip his bulge through his jeans and he grunts, pulling his lips from mine. He moves until they find the column of my neck and he peppers kisses up and down there.

"You-" kiss "–are–" kiss "–beautiful." Kiss.

His hands are everywhere. They light me on fire. For a moment I forget what I am doing, but a throat clearing reminds me.

I make an overdramatic screech to mask the noise of his keys going into my pocket.

"Go home!" an older woman barks at us as she gets into her car and drives away.

Grayson offers a sheepish look. "Go on then."

He helps me off the car and pushes me towards the bathroom. It is a one stall, and I can hear as he takes up post outside of it.

I don't hesitate. There is a window in this cramped space, it will be a tight fit, but as quietly as possible, I open it. Years of going out through windows onto the roof offers me support now as I lift up and through it.

Auggie's hoodie catches and I make the regretful decision to leave it behind to not attract attention. I land gracefully on the other side, but my white shirt shines like a beacon in the darkness.

I creep around the corner, my heart pounding in my chest.

I can see Grayson leaning against the door, tapping anxiously on his jeans. When he turns around to the bathroom to knock, I leap out of my hiding space. Unlocking the car and jumping inside.

"Sunday, no!"

I'm sorry Grayson.

My heart is pounding in my chest. I have to hold back tears. He doesn't deserve me twisting his emotions. Using him like I did. But I need to get these answers, I need to see for myself what's going on. *What else* are they *hiding from me?*

Because even though what they have told me feels like it is a lot, I instinctually know there is more.

I don't stop as I reverse out of the lot and speed off to Julia's. It's time to get some answers.

I need to see Julia, she is my friend. I can trust her.

And even more so? There is something intrinsically tugging me towards her. As if these actions aren't my own but a compulsion I cannot deny.

I can see Grayson sprinting after me, but then he comes to a sudden stop.

I will never get the look of his face out of my mind.

The betrayal, anger, confusion.

But most of all, the terror.

I blink back tears as I race down the road in Grayson's stolen car.

August 14th

Her Day to Die

My phone continues to ring next to me as I drive away, but I don't answer it.

When I am less than a mile away from Julia's house, I think of just throwing it out the window, not telling them where I went.

But that is stupid. Stupider than this irrational decision I made.

Why am I doing this again? Why did I not at least tell them where I am going?

I need to talk to Grayson.

I pick it up.

"Listen close, Sunday. You have made a decision that is not going to end well." Grayson's voice is cool, calm. "Where are you headed this time?"

What does he mean *this time?* I think about it for a moment. I want to lie, but I decide against it. Something is pushing at my psyche; some nagging feeling is urging me to trust him. To trust the O'Briens. Even if they have been lying to me. "Going to Julia's."

Grayson lets out a heavy hopeless sigh into the phone. "I should have known! I should have stopped you. Do you know what the definition of insanity is?" He doesn't wait for an answer. "Making the same decision over and over and fucking over again and expecting different results!" he shouts into my ear.

I'm close to her house, I can see the car from earlier. It's parked in the street. Lights are on inside. "I haven't done anything over and over again, what are you talking about?"

"You stupid, idiot girl. We try to keep you alive, but you keep dying! Ninety-nine deaths. I've watched you die ninety-nine times before this."

His words snap through the strings that have been tugging me incessantly towards Julia.

I slam on the brakes. "What are you talking about?"

"You're caught in an endless loop, Sunday, and no matter what we do, we can never get you past today. You always die either before today or on this date. On Tripp and Axel's birthday."

"That's not possible." But even as I say the words, it's as if everything finally clicks into place. Every creepy feeling, the unending déjà vu, inherently expecting the other shoe to drop.

The apprehension.

"How do you think we always knew where you were? How do you think we could just guess what you were going to do? You had already done it! Sometimes there was a bit of variation, we could alter it a bit. But no matter what, you will die today."

Ice is rushing through my veins to my head. My vision blurs. "But—"

"You made a wish on that shooting star. To be reunited with the ones you love."

Goosebumps form all across my skin, how could he possibly know that?

"Well, we did too; Darius, Axel, and I knew what Tripp and Auggie had gotten into, we suspected it wasn't an accident at all and we wished to keep you safe. For some reason we can remember every timeline, but you can't. It's maddening!"

A thought strikes, the day of the memorial when I was going to walk home. "The lightning?"

"You died the first time from that. OD'd at the party. Falling where the car accident was. Drowning in the river. Suffocated in a barrel. Stabbed underneath the restaurant at the marina. You have died in so many different ways. But there was one constant–if you made it to today? You would be murdered. *Shot.*"

My head is throbbing, I am parked in the middle of the street.

He has to be lying to me, trying to get me to come back, but then why does it feel so true? Why can some part of my subconscious feel like what he is saying actually happened to me? Like it's a memory that I can virtually touch but is just out of my reach. "Why didn't you just tell me?" The words are a weak whisper.

"You never listen. You don't care! Now please. Please, whatever you do, don't go into the house. Don't meet up with Julia. This isn't going to end well. Please come back to me. Before it's too late. Please, I'm begging you. I love you Sunday."

My mind is reeling that I don't quite process everything he has just said. I am still not certain I believe him, but when I look up, I realize it's too late.

"Come on out, Miss Sunday."

August 14th

GRAYSON

The call disconnects and Grayson throws it onto the ground. Axel is already on the way, but it will be too late.

They're always too late.

They can never keep her alive past today.

He had lived years with Sunday in this loop, but she was blissfully unaware. While he and his brothers were forced to restart the pain of another lifetime.

It always rewound to the morning of the memorial.

After they made their god damn wish under the falling star.

Slowly, the three of them fell further in love with the naïve, sweet, blissfully unaware girl, breaking each of their hearts time and time again.

The rumbling of Darius's truck sounds and he looks up. Axel is driving. He wrenches open the door. "Where is Darius?"

"Trying something new, he took my bike. She always dies at the fucking 'accident' site when she goes to Julia's."

"But we don't know that!" Grayson's anger simmers to the surface. He thought this time might be different. That she might actually make it. He allowed himself to hope for a future. He jumps into the truck and slams the door.

Axel speeds away.

"I'm going to the same spot, and if not, then we will just have to do this all over again."

"I can't." Grayson's voice breaks and he presses his sweaty forehead against the cool window. "I can't keep losing her. I can't watch her die in my arms again. I can't see her dead body again. The last time practically broke me. When we pulled the lid off the barrel and there she was, crammed into it. At her favorite goddamn place." Grayson can't keep his emotions under control, and he starts punching the inside of the truck.

"I know." Axel keeps his focus on the road. "I love her, you know? I fell in love with her about the fifth go round. I already cared about her through the letters Tripp wrote me when I was locked away. He made me promise to take care of her if anything happened to him. To be the man she deserved. She is too fucking good, too stubborn, too much of everything. But she cares about us. About all of us. If not this time, we will get past today. We will. We have to."

Grayson doesn't acknowledge the words. He doesn't want to admit that he was in love with Sunday before this even began. That he knew how wrong it was to have a fantasy about his teenage neighbor. How he purposefully distanced himself from her. How he was beginning to suspect it was his fault she never trusted them. Maybe he was the reason she couldn't make it past today.

But this was the first time she had brought him to the space center. It gave him a sliver of promise. That maybe this time would really be different.

They were almost there. Almost to the scene where it all began. Where Tripp and Augustus were run off the road.

Axel makes the turn and the last of Grayson's hope flees his body.

A single street light flickers above. Darius made it before them, but it makes no difference. He is kneeling over a girl with a halo of curls. There is crimson seeping into the ground below her.

Grayson hears the desperate cry that Axel lets out but he pays it no mind. The truck hasn't made it to a complete stop before he is jumping out the door.

August 14th

Darius

He knew it would happen. He knew better than to expect anything different. But love could do crazy things.

Sunday, his wildflower.

Darius rubs the tattoo across his chest as he takes off on the motorcycle. After her tenth death, they realized that she couldn't make it past today, Axel and Tripp's birthday. Now on every timeline since, he gets the date tattooed over his chest as a reminder. After her twenty-second death, he added the wildflowers to it. The pain of his brother and Auggie's death felt further and further away, but hers was always a storm cloud over their heads.

Why were they forced to always remember and yet she always forgot? Was it because she was the one dying? Her wish was being fulfilled, but theirs wasn't? The opposing wishes forcing them into this endless loop?

He didn't understand it, but it didn't change anything.

Usually they had a plan, track her phone, use a past timeline, or follow the clues. But then they never made it to her in time. That wouldn't be the case with this timeline.

Darius is determined to go off script.

The gun in his jeans presses against him as he leans on the motorcycle.

He's nearly there. He will make it.

He has to.

August 14th

Her Day to Die

Come on out, Miss Sunday.

The phone falls from my shoulder as I turn to look at the man brandishing a gun at me. The window is closed, but I have no doubt that it will stop my imminent death.

"Slowly." I expected Maxwell, maybe even Mark.

"Rayden, what are you doing?" The words come out less harsh than I wish for them to be. A series of bombs has been dropped on me progressively in the last several minutes.

I was living a death cycle? A groundhog's day? But I didn't even know it?

"Now." Rayden's typical cool voice is full of menace as he yanks the door open.

In one swift motion he pulls me to my feet. I don't fight him. He has a gun, he's nearly twice my size.

"What are you doing?" I try to meet his eyes, but they are pitch black.

He pushes me towards the car parked outside Julia's house.

"Where is Julia?" I ask, trying to catch anything as we march to his car.

He opens the trunk. "Get inside." He doesn't wait. He simply pushes me in.

Right on top of a body.

I start to scream, but he covers my mouth. "She served her purpose. Now shut the fuck up."

The trunk slams shut and I am left alone in the darkness with only my thoughts, pain, and Julia.

Her lifeless body is underneath me. I can feel the heat of her skin, but she isn't moving. Isn't breathing.

I failed her. I never even looked for her. I just let her be taken into whatever the fuck this is and then she was used to lure me.

What would have happened if I followed her earlier?

I already know the answer though; we would both be lying in this trunk, in a pool of our own blood.

But isn't that how this is going to go anyways? We're both going to be dead?

"Where are you taking me?" I yell through the trunk. I try to disassociate from my skin. I'm not touching Julia. That isn't her blood seeping into my white shirt.

He doesn't answer and after an eternity passes in the darkness of the trunk, the smell of copper enveloping me, we finally come to a stop.

A moment later and he's whipping open the trunk. "Now be a good fucking Sunday and get over to the edge."

A light flickers above, a sense of déjà vu clouds me, and all of a sudden, I am not in this moment. I am in a similar one but different. Memories circulate through me. I pant, trying to catch my breath.

I look behind me. At where Tripp and Auggie went off the road. Correction—where they were forced off the road to their deaths below.

"Why?" I ask. "I haven't done anything!"

Rayden still won't meet my eyes. "You're a loose cannon, too many men fall into the falsity of your innocence. You aren't going to be the reason we get shut down. This operation is too valuable. And I'm sorry to say, you just aren't. Now jump off the ledge like the obedient Sunday you are."

I can tell Rayden has made his mind up. Grayson's words echo around my brain.

I'm going to die today.

I won't let him get off easily. I won't be jumping to my death below.

Before I can register or even think if it's a good idea, I am sprinting away. My gut picks a direction and I just go. And go. And go.

"That's far enough."

Bang.

Thud.

Bang.

Thud.

August 14th

Darius

The gun drops from Darius's hand.

Rayden falls to the ground.

He rushes over to his wildflower.

She's face down in a pool of her own blood.

His own pounds in his ears, his hands shake in anxiety.

He doesn't even look up as he hears the sound of a vehicle approaching. She can't die. He can save her.

He looks for the wound, swallowing down bile as he moves her hair coated in wet dark crimson.

"Darius, we have to go, they can't catch us here. They'll lock us up and throw away the key. You killed him. We have to go and wait for this to restart." Axel rushes to his side, his voice is monotone. Emotionless.

Darius pushes away Sunday's curls and he finally spots it. "Her shoulder." Hope ignites in his belly, a spark of possibilities. This is new, she had never been shot there before.

"What?" Grayson is kneeling beside them now, he leans forward, finding what Darius had. "Just her shoulder? But this never happened before... What changed? Is she... is she going to make it?" His voice pitches in swelling emotion.

The sound of sirens ignites into the air. "I called them," Darius states, trying to maintain his composure. He would need it for the next few steps. "I knew this time would be different. You two need to leave. Axel take the gun, get rid of it. Figure this out. I'm not leaving her side until they make me. Find her at the hospital. It's going to be okay, I can feel it."

Grayson and Axel look like they want to argue, but Darius pushes them both away, keeping his eyes on Sunday.

"Go! Axel can't be caught here and Grayson, they'll lock you up or kill you. I have a chance. Please, Sunday needs to wake up to someone. She needs protection." The words seem to finally knock sense into them and Axel reaches down taking the gun Darius dropped.

They don't say anything else. Axel grabs hold of Grayson and offers Darius an unreadable look before driving as far and as fast as he can away.

Darius has an idea, something that might just help him. This town is corrupt but the one thing about that? They want to keep the underbelly hidden from the public. He quickly sets up his phone camera on a live feed. He isn't sure it will be enough to keep him alive, to get Sunday the help she needs, to keep him safe. But he can hope.

It isn't two minutes later that the sirens approach from the opposite direction that Axel and Grayson made their retreat.

"Show us your hands!"

An officer rushes to Rayden, but Darius can see his head shaking.

Dead.

Darius's hands shake, this is the first timeline he had killed someone himself. It was always left to Axel or Grayson. Another change.

Darius does as told, lifting his hands and staring down the sheriff. "She's bleeding out, she needs a medic." He tries to keep the unease out of his voice, but Sunday hasn't moved since he found her.

"I don't fucking care! What have you done?!" The sheriff is a bulky man, full of anger and distrust. He keeps his gun pointed on Darius as he slowly walks over.

Darius can tell the moment he sees the camera.

"Fuck! Get her some help!"

Thank fuck. It worked to get Sunday help, but would it work for him?

The ambulance has just arrived.

They drag Darius away from Sunday, taking him into custody, but he doesn't care because he is able to see through the window of the back of the police squad as they connect her to the equipment. Hear as it beats to the tune of her heart. Feel as the day shifts. Instinctually, he knows a new timeline solidifies.

They won't be going through this again. She is finally going to make it past today.

Make it past her day to die.

It is *not* her day to die.

Darius watches as the woman he loves is driven away in an ambulance, readying himself to face whatever comes his way, even with the anxiety of all the new thousands of *what ifs* that are forming as he marches on this new timeline.

He can't help but feel relief. He has finally escaped this hell they had been caught in for what was the equivalent of years.

Above, a star falls from the sky.

He doesn't think.

He makes a wish.

About the Author

Yay you made it to the end of book one!!

I have one promise, every series I write will end in a HEA, but the path to it? Well, that will always be a bumpy ride.

Please feel free to stalk me for updates on all my projects. Below is a QR code to take you to my Linktree.

Sneak Peak

Come Inside

Synopsis

Yara runs a company called Darkest Desires. A dating site for those with particular interests.

Because of that she has always received unwanted attention from a vast majority of men.

Including one particularly nasty stalker.

Undeterred by his escalating threats, Yara decides it's time to delve into her own wants and needs.

She finds the perfect match on her list of new potential clients.

Except she probably should have vetted the man a bit better... there's something oddly familiar about him...

Prologue

Yara stepped under the shower's hot mist. She wasn't sure if this was a mistake or not.

She was anxious. Nervous. Excited.

The flurry of emotions were caused by her plans.

They were simple.

By the end of the night Yara would be filled with cum, by a man twice her age.

Chapter One: Yara

I had been told my entire life that I was beautiful, a perfect angel, sexy personified.

For awhile I believed it, even after everything I was put through, but then every time I looked in the mirror, I would find something I didn't like.

My uneven knees, my stomach that would never flatten, the fat on my cheeks.

A new scar. A purple bruise. A broken bone.

The more compliments that were bestowed onto me, the more I hated myself. The more I believed I would never live up to the expectations.

The more my mind rebelled. Until a particularly awful experience back home left me a broken mess.

I could no longer ignore the deformities that covered my body. A testament to my childhood.

Now my mirrors stay covered, and I hide myself in loose dark clothes. Away from the world's watchful eye. Away from men's leering stares. Away from my own gaze.

SAGE RELLEANNE
Dark
Why Choose
Romance
Come
Inside
YARA'S DARKEST DESIRES 1